The Lost Revelation

Also by DH Parsons

The 60s
Life ain't Nothin' but a Slow Jazz Dance
Not Exactly What I Was Expecting
1967 San Francisco:
My Romance with the Summer of Love
The Muse: Coming of Age in 1968

Lifestyle and Inspirational
Eat Yoga!
Book of Din

All available on Amazon

The Diary
of **Mary**
Bliss
Parsons
Volume 2

The Lost Revelation

D H Parsons
Elise R. Brion

The Lost Revelation

Second Edition

This edition contains considerably more material and deeper insights than the previous version.

Copyright 2021 by DH Parsons

Editing, layout, and design by Susan Bingaman, Bliss-Parsons Publishing, Columbia, MO

Bliss-Parsons Institute, founded by DH Parsons, is devoted to the exploration and expression of Truth, with the intent to guide as many people as possible toward Right Living and the healing of spirit, soul, and body.

All rights reserved

ISBN: 978-1-948553-18-6
Library of Congress Control Number applied for.

Contents

PREFACE

My name is DH Parsons. I am an artist, a former school administrator, a teacher of art and history, an author, an ordained minister and church pastor, the founder of the Bliss-Parsons Institute, and a ninth great-grandson of Mary (Bliss) Parsons and her husband, Joseph.

Joseph and Mary Parsons were among the founders of the town of Northampton, Massachusetts. Joseph rose to prominence in Springfield and Boston, as well. A series of events led to accusations of witchcraft against Mary in 1656. Joseph took legal action and successfully defended Mary against the slanderous gossip, but the rumors persisted. In 1675, Mary was arrested, imprisoned, and brought to trial—this time with the added charge of murder by witchcraft. Once again, her defense was successful, and she was declared innocent.

After the trial, Mary and Joseph established residence in Springfield, where Joseph died just eight years later. Even though there were no further accusations against her, rumors and suspicion always pointed to Mary whenever anything unexplainable occurred. The whispers of witchcraft would plague her until her death at age eighty-five.

The historical facts of the life of Mary Bliss Parsons are easily found with a quick search of the internet. What is not so readily available are the details concerning her True nature and history. *Volume One* of *The Diary of Mary Bliss Parsons: The Strong Weet Society* fills in the gaps in the record of Mary's life and explains her nature and mission here on Earth.

Introduction to Volume Two

Mary ended *Volume One* by delivering a final appeal regarding the imminent destruction of the planet:

> *The End Plan is very simple. It's much like Annie's original plan. We, the Family Triad, combined with the other Strong Weet, have to do what we have to do. And they, the people of this Earth, have to do what they have to do. It's as simple as that. It all comes down to the fact that this world is in peril, and unless the remaining Strong Weet who are still out there among our readers come forth, all will be lost. Remember that GOD, THE ALL, the Creator—will not save the Earth unless the humans participate. That is the key to the Earth's survival.*
>
> *This is a dark comedy, Din. It has a deeper meaning, and the readers of this book will either help us in our quest or the countdown to survival—or destruction—will begin. There is no more to say.*

Volume One was about how I Awakened to my true identity and the lessons I needed to learn to reintegrate with my incredible family.

Volume Two takes the story a step further and reaches out to others who are aware, at least on a subliminal level, of forces and realms beyond our perception. These others may even feel that our world now stands at the brink of either oblivion or Paradise. As with all the books in this series, this one includes details that will Awaken those who desire a more active role in determining the fate of Earth.

It is not necessary to read *Volume One* to understand the material presented in *Volume Two*. Still, there is much in it that explains who we (Annie, Mary, and Din) are, where we come from, and why we are here and forms the foundation for what comes later. This information is the key to unlocking the final stages of your Awakening. Without it your education will be incomplete.

Mary's Diary is not a work of fiction. Every word is Truth. Every prophecy is real, and the future of Earth depends on how many people believe them and what action they take because of them. Will this planet be blessed for all eternity or will it be annihilated according to God's Great Plan for the End Times.

✱✱✱

Volume One described the Seeding of Earth under the direction of the Mother of Humanity. It also explained that Mother H is not a goddess but is an energy entity far mightier than the imaginary deities of Earth. Mother H is the energy force used by God's Holy Spirit to sustain and control life throughout the universe. She is more akin to what a human might imagine an angelic being to be. That idea may upset a lot of people who currently revere the goddesses described in various mythologies and history books. Still, Truth is Truth, and the Truth is that Mother H has never been accurately portrayed in human culture but has been misrepresented through the ages, resulting in the multitude of ridiculous versions of her seen in this day and age.

The Lost Revelation

Centuries ago, humanity received the most significant revelation ever shared. It is the Key to Life on Earth and, indeed, throughout the universe. It is the key to success, the key to health, the key to wisdom, the key to survival, the key to everything. Over the centuries, this revelation was forgotten—distorted by the chaos of time, buried in piles of dogma, opinion, false prophecy, and confusion. Never really lost—it has always been in plain view—but for some reason, no one *sees* it anymore.

The prophecy is again revealed on the pages of this book and with its restoration comes one final chance for the human species to survive. One final chance to regain honor. One last opportunity to reach for the stars.

When we refer to "humans," "human beings," or the "human species," we mean all humans of all races and colors, religions, and cultures. We do not recognize or acknowledge any differences. We see only humans. Our books are for all.

This is *The Lost Revelation.*

A History Lesson

Approximately 3.5 million years ago, a civilization named Annica was SEEDED on this planet by Beings of a higher energetic frequency than those who would later be called human beings. These higher-energy Beings were from a world located directly behind the star, Alcyone, in what Earth astronomers call the Pleiadian Star Cluster. The proper name of the planet is Hectarus, named after the Mother of Humankind, the Energy Being of Creation. This Energy Being is the ultimate Creative Force of God and is also the Mother of the Spirit Beings of Mary and me, Din.

The Mother of Humankind, or Mother H as we call her, created the birthing process and, as such, is the Mother of all humans on Earth. Mother H used her own Energy to form the Created Beings, Mary and Din, and they are indeed her children. Created Beings are not grown within a womb and brought forth knowing nothing but their generation. They are ancient energies who chose to JUMP from life to life to make sure that The Great Plan for the Development of Humanity is in harmony with the Will of God, the Creator.

The Created Beings' original purpose was to SEED the millions of planets in this universe so that the Creation Frequencies of Unconditional Love and Truth would be broadcast throughout this universe and its neighbors. There are only three Created Beings on Earth at this time. Din and Mary are two. The third is Annie, an eternal Energy Being of Great Power who became the daughter of Din and Mary by the command and direction of

The All. If you have read *Volume One* of Mary's Diary you will understand how all of this came to be. If not, don't worry, as it will become clear as you continue in this volume.

It seems, however, that Earth culture has turned its back on the original intent of *The All*. Humanity has deviated from the purpose of Truth. Today we find ourselves saturated not with the frequencies of Truth and Order, Love and Goodwill, but with human-imagined emotions of greed, hatred, anger, jealousy, rage, and many others, resulting from a willful disconnection from God. God is deeply distressed by this detachment, for which there are only two possible solutions. One is that Earth and all its inhabitants are destroyed, scattered into space, and forgotten forever. The second solution, or what Mother H calls the Primary Option, is to save the Earth from annihilation.

The Primary Option directs the Created Beings to initiate focused Hectaran frequencies with the power to change the hearts and minds of humans. The effect of those frequencies is to "reset" humans so that they can enjoy lives filled with Unconditional Truth and Order. God has, however, made the condition that there must be a portion of humans who are willing to help save this world from destruction before implementing the Primary Option.

Two groups of humans who will help make the rest of the population aware of the situation and rally their support are the Secondary Weet and the Support Weet. These individuals all carry at least a small amount of ancestral genetic material linking them to Earth's original inhabitants. Another group of individuals, the Strong Weet, is directly related to the seven Founders placed on Earth at the time of the Seeding. They have much more power than the Secondary and Support Weet.

The number of Strong Weet on Earth is set at ten. In addition to the Family Triad—the three original Created Beings, Din, Mary, and Annie,—there are seven Earth humans. Those seven, along with fourteen Secondary Weet and numerous Support Weet remain to be discovered among the readers of Mary's Diary. Coded keywords and phrases appear throughout the text of this Diary. They will prompt the Awakening of all Weet who read them. Not all descendants of the Founders are Weet. Many of them have yielded to the temptations of shallow human culture and have no genuine concern for the well-being of this world or its inhabitants. The execution of The Great Plan will not include those descendants.

The first volume of *The Diary of Mary Bliss Parsons, The Strong Weet Society*, began by discussing the Salem Witch trials and Mary's relationship to that era. It was made clear early on that Mary was not a witch, and the so-called magic that appears to emanate from Mary, Din, or Annie has nothing to do with magic at all but with physics and Universal Laws created by God. The word "Weet" has nothing to do with witchcraft. Weet are Beings endowed with greater sensitivities, awareness, and abilities than the ordinary beings who populate all worlds in all universes. The powers of energy frequency and change that Weet might utilize have nothing to do with so-called witches. This, too, was explained in *Volume One*. The supernatural is often confused with the unknown, but magic is merely undiscovered science. What humans often label as wizardry is simply a matter of physics. It might help to remember that the Earthly idea of alien is inaccurate as well. Nearly every race of beings found in this universe, regardless of the star system in which they reside, closely resembles Earth human beings. A hundred different so-called aliens from a hundred different planetary groups show only minimal variation in appearance. Races and religions do not exist anywhere else in the universe either. There is only one race, human, and only one religion, God. These concepts were also thoroughly discussed in *Volume One* but will be revisited in this volume as well.

Emotions are a different story. For uncountable eons, the inhabited planets throughout the vastness of space have evolved emotionally. Over time, the baser emotions have become more frequently expressed than the purer emotions, threatening to disrupt the balance of the universe. Observing this, God allowed the Created Beings, who preside over this and all other universes, to place a countdown clause in The Great Plan for each of their inhabited planets. God will activate this clause should He deem it necessary.

Mother H is in total agreement with the countdown clause. The past hundred years on Earth have seen very few times of joy and virtually none of Unconditional Love. There have been short bursts of peace and contentment, but none of pure Unconditional Love.

When we speak of base emotions, we mean jealousy, greed, anger, hatred, envy, false pride, religious zealotry, covetousness, and so forth. All emotions are the product of the ego. Love is not an emotion, nor is joy, or peace. These are Hectaran frequencies, or vibrations created by God and implanted in the hearts of human beings. It is more accurate to call them forces. Anger, sadness, hate, vengeance, and the like are not natural or human. They are the way of the lesser evolved beings inhabiting the five darker worlds. By holding onto these deadly intoxicants, people not only remain imprisoned by their egos but secure their own ultimate demise.

✳✳✳

Jesus the Christ, born in human form on the Earth, was the first opportunity offered by God, His Father, for humans to reclaim their original state of purity. Jesus did not come to this planet to be the leader of a new religion. He came to awaken Truth in the hearts of humans. The intent was for humanity to embrace His teachings fully. Instead, humans once again took Truth and made it into religion. That was an act of rebellion against God and cemented the pattern of negative emotional thought firmly in the minds of everyone on Earth.

One last Hope is that Earthlings still have the free will given to them when they were created, along with the ability to help the Strong Weet by following the Weet guidelines of behavior described in the closing chapters of this book.

The Family Triad has been returning to Earth lifetime after lifetime to assist in maintaining a balance of Unconditional Love and Unconditional Truth in the face of wrong thinking. Because of their dedication and devotion, humanity has been allowed to continue. We have, however, come to the end of that time. There will be no more lifetimes in human bodies for the Family Triad. Of course, that may also be true for every living being here. The countdown clock is ticking.

Even though the Created Beings are fully capable of solving the problem without the Weet's input, God will not allow them to do so. Human beings must be a part of this if only to show that they desire to perpetuate their species.

The following pages present concise lessons and examples that give insight into how humans can aid the work of the Family Triad to ensure the perpetuation of the human species and the planet Earth.

End of the boring introductory history lesson.

***

Please read this volume of *Mary's Diary* carefully. Many of the Weet necessary to help the Family Triad save Earth will Awaken to their identity through these words.

I need to get on with the complicated life I've JUMPED into this time around, so if you will excuse me —

This will indeed be the last Earth life, Father.

I hope so, Annie.

Whether we save this planet or destroy it, our work here will be finished, and we can all return Home.

There are many other planets out there that need our guidance, Annie.

Hectarus needs us even more. Your Higher Authority calls — after you have completed this task.

What a comforting thought that is after all these years of JUMPING in and out of human bodies.

Grandma H has asked that one of us explain to the readers how it is that you are the great-grandson of Mary and have JUMPED in and out of bodies both before and after you JUMPED into Joseph's body in the seventeenth century.

Didn't we explain that in *Volume One?*

We did not. Not completely.

But how in the world can we explain something so complex and so unfamiliar to humans in a language that doesn't have the vocabulary to describe it?

We must try to show that such a wonderful thing can, indeed, occur. As you well know, Earthlings have been locked into their concept of linear time for eons. Many engaging human minds have come and gone, and humanity has virtually nothing to show for it. What humans considered to be progress and technology are merely the juvenile results of what I've heard you refer to as "piddling away their years on simplistic nonsense."

If we can give the readers images throughout this book of the truly wonder-filled possibilities available in this galaxy, perhaps it will encourage them to reach for the stars instead of their TV remotes.

I believe you are right. It may be their only chance to save the planet, but the remaining years don't give them much time to achieve inter-dimensional travel or learn to JUMP to and from Hectarus in the twinkling of an eye.

I know. We'll have to limit them for a while to only a vision of the possibilities. If The Great Plan ends successfully for this species, we will share more with them.

I can't help but feel a little frustrated, though. All of this nonsense should never have happened. From the moment we began this world, our influence should have advanced rapidly.

Instead, a host of evil-natured alien beings snuck onto this planet and hid among the humans. They were able to sway the population and cause them to introduce their own seeds of doubt, greed, and negativity. We did not stop these invaders from star systems other than our own, and we should have.

Now we must do our best to change human hearts back to what is good and pure. The task will be difficult. Earthlings have so fooled themselves by their belief that they could eliminate their problems through politics, social programs, and money, all of which are really the cause of the fix they are in today. We must somehow teach them to release those primitive ideas. We must also introduce this species to our higher frequencies so that their conscious minds will be more open to receiving Truth instead of fiction.

That is where our Weet come in.

It is. But first, I will explain how you have been able to do what you have done by JUMPING into many human lives.

I was hoping you would.

Annie explains JUMPING into a Life

Dearest reader, you are no doubt aware of the concept of reincarnation. That is where this lesson on Father's ability to move about from life to life begins. As you know, reincarnation is the human belief that when a physical body dies, the energy and awareness, or spirit, of that body does not come to an end. A human spirit leaves the old body and transfers to a new body to live again as a different physical person. It will reside in its new body until the physical brain dies and the process of reincarnation begins again.

This idea is just a human guess about what happens after physical death. It is a fashionable philosophy regarding the afterlife, but it is not correct. Keep in mind that I am speaking of Father in this lesson and not of mortal humans. Father does not reincarnate. He never has — on this planet or any other. He is a Created Being and is not subject to the same physical laws that govern humans or any other species in this universe. JUMPING *into a human body is a complex process done with the permission of the human occupying the chosen body. This practice results in the melding of the Created Being's Spirit with the Spirit of that human and is used to manage the progress of the Great Plan. When the task is complete, the Created Being* JUMPS *out of the body and is immediately back home on Hectarus. The human is left alone in his body, enriched by the experience of having shared it with the Created Being.*

This sharing of bodies has been a regular practice for eons to allow the Created Beings to gently — and sometimes not so gently — maneuver humanity back to the proper course of its development.

Father has JUMPED *into dozens of bodies and has influenced some of the most famous and notorious humans at critical moments in Earth history. Several times, The Great Plan required both Father and Mother's presence, and they were able to work together as husband and wife on Earth. When Mother needed to work as Mary back in the 1600s, Father chose to be Joseph, her husband. In that Massachusetts life, the body of Joseph died before Mary's body. Since Father's task was complete, he* JUMPED *out of Joseph's body and waited back home on Hectarus for Mother to complete her Earth life. Mother's job was much more complex than Father's, so she stayed longer. Her role in that life was to begin preparations to gather the Strong Weet back into the fold so that all would be ready for the final stages of The Great Plan. She had to acquire a reputation as a witch to attract and Awaken the Strong Weet in the twenty-first century.*

***

She did a good job of it too, Annie. My job back then as Joseph was to use my wealth and social standing to protect Mary from the punishment that witchcraft accusations could bring. It was a close thing. If our timing had been off and we had shown up ten or fifteen years later, it would have been difficult to escape the frenzy of the Salem Witch Trials.

I also had to make sure that Mary had a child to assure that there would be a genetically-related body I could JUMP into down the line. When Mother H released her ball lightning, as described in *Volume One*, my GLOW ignited inside this current conscious mind, and my Awakening began.

The Strong Weet and the Secondary Weet will understand. What we need to do now is give our readers some background and few clear images to make the Diary come alive for them as they read about unfamiliar people and places.

How do we do that?

I had in mind that you should JUMP *back to Hectarus for a short time and describe a few things.*

What kind of things?

It doesn't matter. See where you land and describe it in detail. Let the readers see Hectarus through your eyes.

I'm pretty good at winging it, Annie, but what are you going to be doing while I'm back Home?

I've got a ton of things piled up that need attention.

Well, while you're un-piling things, see what you can do about sending me another Strong Weet or two. There's a lot to do, and we could use all the help we can get.

I'll do my best. There are more out there that haven't yet Awakened, and only a few Secondary Weet have come forward so far. Don't forget that all but two will be using fictitious names.

I hate having to do that. It won't bother the readers, but it will confuse the heck out of me, trying to keep them all straight.

There is concern that family members might be upset by this knowledge and that friends might be jealous. Activity on the social media sites is increasing rapidly, and there are people there who would ridicule them and try to drag them through the mud.

You're right, of course.

It's best to keep their identities a secret. Don't forget Mother H's Laws for Growth of Power.

You mean the four principles that Earth witchy people stumbled on a few years ago and watered down so that they would better serve their egos?

I do.

Annie explains the Laws for the Growth of Power

TO KNOW. TO WILL. TO DARE. TO BE SILENT. Human so-called witches think they invented these, but God planted knowledge of them in the human heart and mind to generate a sense of strength and confidence within individuals. They have nothing to do with witchcraft or magic. As we have previously explained, witchcraft and magic are inventions from the minds of Earth humans.

Mother H initially designated these principles as To Be, To Create, To Allow, and To Remain Silent. Some humans come close with their interpretations, but by not crediting God and ignoring Mother H's instructions, they removed the power from them. The original focus of these Principles was much more exacting and demanding.

To a person trying to practice witchcraft these days, "To Know" means that one must acknowledge that there is more to the universe than meets the eye and that there is a more potent source of power available which, if accessed, could be used to accomplish all manner of things. If you think about it, this is a statement of a negative rather than a positive. It actually implies that the so-called witches know there is a more potent power source they could use if only they could figure out how. That's a big if, which further implies that they cannot tap into it.

Rather than "To Know," the Hectaran would say, "To Be," meaning, "I possess all Truth." There is no speculation on Hectarus. Truth is known by all. That is why results are easy to achieve even though magic does not exist there. There are no incantations, herbs, candles, phases of the moon, altar tools. None of those things have ever existed back Home. Results simply happen. Whenever one desires something, regardless of what that might be, they make it happen. Creative acts on Hectarus are an everyday occurrence. No spells are necessary, and wannabe witches are non-existent. The only requirement is that the desired act must coincide with God's will, or it will not be allowed. That is the point the witch people intentionally ignore.

Another reason for the failure of witchcraft here on Earth lies in the fact that witches do not believe in God.

They subscribe to and aggressively demand service from a pantheon of imaginary beings. At best, they visualize a higher power or higher being as some sort of universal consciousness that arises from the collective minds of human beings. It is no wonder their magic does not work. Success comes only when The True and Only GOD, the God of the Trinity, is present and acknowledged. The so-called witches of modern Earth have removed God from the equation.

"To WILL," in its original Hectaran form, is "To CREATE." In the modern, watered-down Earth version, it is no more than a willful human demand. But again, this is a negative statement and not a positive principle. To a Hectaran, it means "make it so." It's a statement of immediate creation. The Hebrew-Christian Bible got it right in the book of Genesis, where it reads, "And God said, Let there be …." (fill in the blank). In essence, God said it, and it was so—rather like Captain Picard from that Star Trek show you like so well, Father. He simply decided on a course of action then said, "Make it so," and it was done.

When God, THE ALL, said, "Let there be light," there was light. Period. The statement represented the immediate act of creation for whatever THE ALL was producing out of nothing. "To CREATE" is used every day by every Being on Hectarus. Of course, the general population uses the command only to create items of necessity and pleasure for their immediate use. The act is somewhat like that of an artist on Earth "creating" an original work from materials previously created by God. A higher form of this principle is used exclusively by God, Mother H, and the Family Triad to produce entire universes from nothing—or to destroy them.

"To DARE" implies to an Earth person some sort of leap

of faith. If one does not dare to take that leap, no magic will take place. On Hectarus, there is no daring, and there is no need for a leap of faith. When you possess ultimate Truth and have the power to create, both daring and faith become unnecessary. Instead, the Hectaran would use the term, To Allow, because God, not humans, is the Creator and the Programmer of all elements. We allow the elements to create the structures we desire, and the elements themselves enable the process.

"To Be Silent" is the most important of all. Modern Earth humans have it nearly right when they say that once you cast a spell or do whatever you are trying to do, you should simply forget about it. Remain silent. To constantly revisit a scenario to change or repeat silly phrases over and over again is to take power away from the action you have already allowed. It is counterproductive.

The truth is that so-called spells cast on this planet simply do not work anyway, so it's useless to waste time on them. There is also a bit of hypocrisy at play here. To suggest that power is taken away from a spell by repeating it contradicts the belief that repeating positive affirmations gives them more power. This point illustrates how the original power and energy introduced to this world has been stripped of God's Truth and turned into a chaotic hodgepodge of nonsense over the years. Most modern witchcraft is nothing more than theater, entertainment, ego, and religious emotion. Quite frankly, many churches are falling into this trap as well. Humans just aren't getting it. The Bible clearly tells humans to stay away from things like witchcraft for two good reasons. First, witchcraft gives no credit to God, and God doesn't like that. Second, even though witchcraft doesn't work, humans are so dull-witted that, at times, their attempts to make it work could get them into trouble or even cause them physical harm.

It's for their own good to just leave it alone.

When a Hectaran envisions results, that is the end of it. Silence naturally follows because there is no need to do or say anything else. It is an immediate thing. To mention it to another is to belittle God's act of creation. Once it is so, that's it. It is as if it has always been so, and there is no need to speak of it. We need to ask no one's permission, and we need not inform anyone of our actions. We answer only to God, which is the essence of what separates the Hectaran from humans. Hectarans believe in and depend totally on God. It is a True relationship. Many humans not only do not believe in God, but they also deny and even curse Him. They invent false gods and goddesses to take His place. All they are really doing is sealing their own sad destiny. Humans were created to worship God, not to misrepresent and defile Him. Here too, the human churches separate themselves from God by what they allow into their worship services. Many of their services have become no different from some pagan services — complicated and meaningless rituals, long-winded prayers, insipid music, costumes, and rigidly-planned programs. They have forgotten that Jesus dressed in a simple robe and sat on a hillside or stood in a boat out in Nature to teach simple things to all who would listen. Christianity must rid itself of the world and return to Christ.

***

Well said, Annie.

Thank you. Now you must be off. I'm sending you to Hectarus to describe our home world for the readers who have not yet heard of it. The task will also be an opportunity to explain more about Grandma H's true nature. We want every human on this planet to know who they are dealing with whenever the Mother of Humanity is mentioned. We want them to have a picture of what she looks like and an accurate idea of her power. When she becomes more involved in the affairs of this world, everyone alive must deal with her. Some will fear and hate her, but some will also love her and want to help her save this planet from destruction. Your descriptions of her will go far to establish and distinguish those two viewpoints. Depending upon how you present Grandma H, the Earthlings will make their decisions, and those decisions will be final. Are you ready to return home?

I don't think I'm ever ready for this. While I'm in physical form, some things are still a shock to my system. Inter-dimensional travel across four hundred and forty light-years of deep space in the time it takes a human heart to beat only once is a little hard to get used to. I'll be glad when I don't have to use this fleshly body to get around in.

This is your last human life. Remember that. After this one, we will all be together back Home.

Forever. No more Earth JUMPS.

No more Earth JUMPS. Together for eternity.

Let's do this.

Din Describes Hectarus

I really can't get used to that. I have yet to find a way to explain how it feels to be there one second and here in the next. How can an interval of time so minutely small seem so endlessly long? How can I sense such massive weight and feather lightness at the same time? How can I possibly feel the compression of a million tons of granite pressing in on me while I am fully aware that the air around me is cool and bright and as weightless as nothing at all? That doesn't make sense. Nothing makes sense when it comes to describing something indescribable. There is no other experience like it.

My brief ordeal is over, and I'm standing here on Hectaran soil. I really think Annie could do a better job describing our home world, but I'll do the best I can.

The sky is a brilliant turquoise blue, all but blinding in its intense clarity. There are no clouds. It never rains on Hectarus, so clouds aren't necessary, although any one of us could create clouds if we wished, just for the ambiance. Here on Hectarus we don't have anything like human emotions, which can be pretty dangerous and detrimental to a society. Sensual moods evoked by things like Sunsets, rainstorms, and the night sky, though, are part of the frequency of Unconditional Love. The night sky here on Hectarus is quite romantic with three multicolored Moons and billions of visible stars, some of which appear to be the same size as Earth's Moon when viewed from the surface of that planet.

We make it rain simply to enjoy the sound the rain makes. I know Mother H loves to create rainstorms, particularly the dramatic ones, complete with lightning and thunder and wild gray clouds that roll through the sky at tremendous speeds. Occasionally she will use such an atmosphere to make a grand appearance, slowly revealing herself from behind the biggest, darkest cloud in a massive form compelling all who see her to gasp and drop to their knees in awe.

I remember the first time I ever saw Mother H in this life—back when I wasn't used to her. It was many years ago, in a dream. Back then, I could only visualize Mother H as I presumed her to be. My image of her took the form of one of those goddesses mentioned in books about Celtic Britain. Whenever I thought anything about her, that's the way I saw her in my head. Even that wasn't a clear image because I didn't really buy into all that goddess stuff anyway. I knew that God used energy to get things done down here, and gods and goddesses were just human ideas invented to give a face to the thing. How do you visualize Energy manifesting as a personified Being? Then I had my dream.

I didn't know it at the time, but Mother H played a little trick on me in that dream. She appeared to me as a wicked-looking witch with dark black hair and lily-white-bordering-on-light-green skin, with a mole on her face, like something out of a Walt Disney cartoon. She wore a black dress, very short. I remember taking note of her perfect thighs—which were what I would expect from a goddess. Here is the exact journal entry relating to my dream:

My First Dream of Mother H

I dreamed that a witch dressed in black floated past a picture window. I was inside a room looking out on a kind of hilly-farmy-country kind of scene. She drifted across the scene from left to right.

I said to someone who was apparently with me in the dream (I have no idea who it was), "Watch! She'll come back. She's—", and then she floated back from right to left. Somehow, I knew she would turn and look at me. She did. She looked me right in the eyes, then smiled and disappeared in a mist.

Her face was hag-like. It should have been frightening, but it wasn't. Earlier that day, I had been studying a book about the history of goddesses in preparation for a part of my master's thesis. I had thought that I would like to have a mental image of the earliest world goddess. Could this have been her? Did she make a special dream appearance just for me?

I think she did. At least, that was my strong impression.

That was the end of the journal entry I wrote immediately after the dream itself. The following day, though, I recalled even more details than I had written the night before.

Then I blinked. I saw the inside of my eyelids as they fluttered just once. I realized I had been dreaming and was now waking up. The inevitable was about to happen, darn it. I didn't want to, but I was about to open my eyes. I did so slowly and against my will. The first ray of morning light brought me back to my own physical, superficial, worldly world.

In that dream, I saw Mother H right in front of me as if she were a totally solid human. This great and wonderful Being whose crooked, sharp teeth showed through her smile, and her breath escaped from her mouth with a warm hiss and smelled like — remember those chewy, white taffy-type candy squares with little green and red jelly things buried in them? Solid sugar with all those nasty additives? My Earth mother used to buy them for me at the market when I was a kid growing up in Tulsa. That's what Mother H's breath smelled like — that white nougat stuff. It was nice. It brought back a sweet childhood memory.

Still in the dream, still looking directly into my eyes, Mother H smiled a smile that melted my heart. I saw a tiny tear slip down her cheek from her left eye, and inside my mind, I clearly heard, "Wake up, baby boy. Wake up." Then she shot backward at a fantastic speed until she disappeared into the mist at the top of the hill in the distance.

I didn't know then that this wonderful green goddess was my ancient Energy Mother or that when she delivered her last order for me to wake up that she was commanding her son to Awaken from his mortal, human dream state and become aware of who he really was. I realize now that my process of Awakening began at that moment. Yes, her dream gift to me was meant to be fun. Mother H isn't really green with pointy teeth. She is Pure Energy, constantly manipulated by the Holy Spirit of God. And yes, it has been a slow process to get to where I am now, but now that I am aware of Truth, I thank God for being patient with me.

****

Where was I before I thought of that dream?

I was speaking about being able to create moods like rainstorms and night skies out of nothing. That's what we do on Hectarus. I'm not in the mood for that sort of thing right now as I gaze out over the meadowland beyond the Temple. I want to see sunshine and feel the warmth of it. I want to see the millions of flowers spread out before me shine their GLOWS as brightly as possible, to the point of blinding these human eyes if they must. I want to carry the memory of their intense color back to the Earth so that I can recall it at any time. If there is one thing I truly miss when I am not here on my Home planet, it is this vista. The view encompasses millions upon millions of flowers eight feet tall or more. Each flower is an individual, sentient being of intense color whose sole purpose is to share the beauty of Light and Joy with the other beings that live here. One of my favorite things to do while I'm here is to float above the ground and look down upon the vast fields of kaleidoscopic color that spread out for hundreds of miles — something like the sunflower fields in my home state of Kansas only far more intense.

Every being on Hectarus, regardless of shape, size, or function, has been given a sacred gift from God to share with all of the others. The Forces of Unconditional Love and Unconditional Truth emanating from God give rise to and sustain these gifts. These two great Forces are central to establishing harmony and happiness in this and all other universes.

Hectarus does not have towns and cities or even continents like Earth. Since the Beings in residence can create their own environments, none of those are necessary. This single large city surrounds the enormous Crystal Temple that sits atop a tall mountain located at its center. Library of Memory and a few other lovely structures used for communal gatherings circle the mountain's base. There are around fifty thousand residents of the city living in dwellings of their own design, many of which are underground. Those living in underground homes can reproduce any scene or environment found outdoors — a beach-side hut, a tree house in a forest, or something entirely imaginary and indescribable. Not only that, but they can change it all on a whim. Regardless of where they choose to live, Hectarans can produce any atmosphere, setting, or situation they want, any time they want it.

I'm looking out across a meadow that extends to the distant horizon. The only breaks in the continuous field of flowers are an occasional lone tree or a stand of thirteen trees placed here and there for purely aesthetic reasons. Trees on Hectarus are much larger than trees on Earth, and one Hectaran tree would be enough to shade an entire acre of land on this planet. The thoughtfully spaced plantings of thirteen trees provide thousands of large parks worldwide for the citizens to enjoy. Each of the thirteen different tree species represents one of the thirteen families of sacred Tree Beings found here at Home. Ten of the species grow on both Hectarus and Earth. The three found only on Hectarus were created by God as a special gift to this sacred world. Trees on Hectarus are fully sentient, have independent personalities, and live life in complete awareness of everything around them. We refer to them using human pronouns. Ten species of Hectaran trees—Pine, Tamarisk, Linden, Oak, Palm, Elm, Maple, Ash, Hawthorn, and Cottonwood—were SEEDED on Earth and other planets across the galaxy. Three trees—the All Tree, the Tree of Truth, and the Tree of the Altar of God—are found only on Hectarus.

At first, there was only one set of the three Hectaran trees. They grew on the Temple grounds shielded from the general population because of their significance to the history of Hectarus. Mother H decided that the people needed to be able to enjoy these trees as well. She approached God, the Father of all trees everywhere, with a request to create three identical trees to be planted in the Temple Park outside the sacred area. God had a better idea. God added replicas of the three sacred trees to every stand of ten across Hectarus.

Mary Bliss Parsons had a stand of thirteen trees in the back of her cottage garden in Massachusetts. She wanted to have a part of her beloved homeland close to her at all times. No one noticed that several of those trees were not native to that region. Nor did they notice that three of those, the sacred trees of Hectarus, did not even exist on Earth. If archaeologists were to dig down where Mary's trees once stood, they just might find a bit of tree DNA that would be impossible to identify.

***

I'm leaving the meadow now and walking around to the Library of Memory on the other side of the temple grounds beside the deep indigo-blue water of our beloved Temple Lake. A long path paved with red basalt winds over the middle of the lake like a bridge and continues on the other side, leading up to the front steps.

The Library of Memory is a beautiful sight to see. The building is only one story above ground, but the four glass walls are fifty feet high. A crystal dome tops the structure, and a tall tower rises from the back corner. It is an architectural masterpiece incomparable to any building on Earth, principally because of the materials used to create it and the various functions of each room housed within.

As with most buildings on Hectarus, the Library of Memory is constructed entirely of Hectaran crystal. Unlike crystal or glass on Earth, Hectaran crystal is not cast or cut. The architect uses his mental will to design, shape, and mold the material, then cause it to appear in its proper place. It is truly a created building, as are the Temple and all other buildings on Hectarus, and all are in a constant state of creation. Like the trees, buildings too, have sentience.

Much of the Library's functional space is below ground. The edifice seen above is just the tip of the iceberg, so to speak, covering only about a hundred acres. Below the planet's surface, a network of tunnels and chambers radiates from the relatively small central structure, fanning out in all directions for hundreds of miles. Similarly, the Crystal Temple alongside the giant meadow extends for over a thousand miles of sub-surface area and contains rooms the size of cities and hallways the length of interstate highways in the United States. Everything is illuminated by what we call star moss that grows anywhere the architect waves a hand.

Even though every room is underground and made of Hectaran Crystal, what greets the eye where the walls should be is not the dirt and rocks of the Hectaran underground but the same view as that seen from the surface of the planet directly above the room. In the case of the Temple, it would be the meadow of flowers. The view from any room in the Library is of the Temple and the Temple grounds, including the lake and the forest directly behind the Library of Memory. Such is the wonder of Hectaran architecture.

I cannot give an account of the rooms and their functions within the Temple and the Library. Some are private and can never be discussed, and the others are so numerous it would take an entire library of books to describe their functions. I will, however, try to clarify a few things.

Our Temple has little to do with the Worship of gods or personal ritual on the part of the population of Hectarus. The only *God* in this and all other universes is GOD, THE ALL, the Trinity of God, Son, and Holy Spirit, exactly as Jesus taught on Earth. God does not demand our worship. He does not need false rituals. Our worship of THE ALL is built into the structure and function of our personal GLOW and expressed through our energy frequency work. We Worship automatically with every breath we take and every move we make. The Temple's primary function is to provide the perfect transmitter for the sacred Creation Frequency emitted by Mother H and directed by the Family Triad. This divine Creation Frequency is what stabilizes and sustains every life form everywhere. It pulsates at regular intervals from deep within the heart of the Temple, projecting signals out through space at faster-than-light speeds. It covers the depth and breadth of the universe in less than a moment. Without this frequency, all life would cease instantly.

There are also secondary frequency chambers throughout the Temple where priests and priestesses of lower or specialized ranks manage and direct energy frequencies. One of the larger rooms in the Temple houses the Central Radiation Stone mentioned in *Volume One* of the *Diary*. Very little energy is used here on Hectarus as we have no machinery or transportation devices. The Central Radiation Stone functions primarily to distribute our energy frequencies for use throughout this universe. A small portion is retained here in the Temple to charge the devices used for healing the human-like beings from other planets who come to our world for physical healing.

The Family Triad meets regularly with Mother H to discuss The Great Plan in the small room at the back of the Temple known as the Family Room. The Creator God will make an appearance occasionally, usually just to let us know that we are loved, and all is well.

A small clearing is located outside at the edge of the Pine Forest about an eighth of a mile behind the Temple and aligned with its center. It is perhaps the most sacred historic spot on the entire planet as it is the site of the replica of Mary's cottage on Earth, complete with her surrounding gardens, the ring of thirteen trees, and the little stream running nearby. Every board, stone, window, nail, and item in the cottage are exact replicas of the original. Every flower and blade of grass in the garden is identical. The only difference is that the cottage here on Hectarus is constructed entirely of crystal, shaped to duplicate Mary's home in Massachusetts.

I'm getting a call in my head from Mary telling me

that I need to hurry this up a bit, but I want to mention a couple more things about the Library of Memory.

The Library has thousands of rooms, many of them filled with copies of important books collected from all over the universe. Much has been written about the Library of Alexandria on Earth, which contained hundreds of scrolls gathered from nearly every country on that world until the time of the library's destruction in 48 BC. The entire library at Alexandria could have fit into a tiny corner of the front reception area of our Library here on Hectarus.

A visitor enters the Library of Memory by climbing the twenty-one wide marble steps up from the red basalt pathway to the massive crystal doors at the top. The doors open with a thought from the visitor to give entry into the immense reception area. A table just inside is occupied by five Library guides who telepathically direct visitors to their desired destination. No impurity or contamination can be allowed to pass beyond the reception area, so everyone must pass through the Waterfall of Purity before proceeding further.

Located at the back of the reception area in the center of a veritable jungle of giant ferns, tropical plants, and even trees, the Waterfall of Purity is beautiful and functional. The water, which is not really water, drifts down from the center of the massive crystal dome that shines into the reception area, onto the waterfall, and into the entrance to the Library rooms behind it. As I said, the water is not really water and is not really wet. It is a form of pure multicolored light energy that feels like a watery mist to anyone who comes into contact with it—kind of like walking through a foggy mist in an English forest. Each tiny droplet is also a prism so that when light from the skylight above strikes the mist, it transforms into a shimmering, shifting veil of rainbow-colored light. During the periods deemed to be "night" on Hectarus, the rays of colored light from the waterfall weave themselves together and stream upward through the rooftop dome and shoot off into space, penetrating every universe and delivering a message of Blessing and Peace from God to every living being.

There are many rooms in the Library of Memory that are particularly notable and worthy of description, but for now, I will focus on just one. Directly behind the Waterfall of Purity and off to one side is the small cave-like entrance into what has commonly become known as the Green Room, as thousands of lush, tropical plants fill the entire space. The famous Palm House at Kew Gardens in London on Earth is a pale imitation by comparison. The purpose of the room is for meditation and contemplation. Small glass tables with seating for one or two tucked into secluded openings in the vegetation throughout the room facilitate that use. It is most pleasant to come to the Green Room after being washed in the Waterfall of Purity. One is brought into a state of complete Peace by the little alcoves' total solitude and the energy emanating from the myriad hues of the color Green. If someone does not want to sit in complete silence, all they have to do is wave a hand over the table, and the table generates music that only they can hear. No one else in the Green Room is disturbed. I have spent many hours in there during my lifetimes, and I can think of little else more calming and revitalizing than the deep silence there.

By the way, music on Hectarus is so different from music on Earth that an Earthling would not recognize it. True music doesn't even exist on Earth. What passes for music there — especially contemporary music — is nothing more than various chaotic frequencies of energy released into the air to interfere with the constructive and supportive energy frequencies streaming from Hectarus to the Earth. The interference is particularly damaging to our Creation Frequency, distorting its original purpose of providing and sustaining life on planet Earth.

Over the past few decades, earthlings have become aware of changes in their environment—temperature fluctuations, shifting storm patterns, melting ice, for example. They have detected a pattern in these changes and have projected that they pose a threat to life on Earth, or at least to civilization as they know it. They have decided that human activity is to blame and have packaged both the effect and the cause as the theory of global warming. Most recently, global warming has attained status as fact rather than theory, and to further promote acceptance of the idea has been relabeled as climate change.

In a way, the earthlings are right; their environment is changing. Earth is a living, breathing organism, and that is to be expected. They are even correct to say that humans are to blame. They are wrong, though, to believe that the cause is as simple as fossil fuel emissions and other forms of air pollution. Floods, droughts, hurricanes, and tornados, as well as earthquakes, volcanoes, and other natural disasters, are caused by one of two things—the evil thoughts and selfish actions billions of Earthlings engage in every moment of every day, and the various manufactured sound waves produced by human beings. Each of these is damaging on its own, but they are devastating in combination. The first, evil thoughts and actions, is well-known and fairly obvious. The second, manufactured sound, requires some explanation.

Earth music produces some of the most disturbing energy frequencies. This manipulation of sound dangerously alters the life energy so meticulously calibrated and sent to Earth by the ranks of Hectaran priests and priestesses. No single type of Earth music is any worse than the others in this regard. All forms of music are equally disruptive — from classical to rock, to rap, to pop, even folk and ethnic music and what passes for country music these days. All of it contributes to the degradation of Nature, and Nature responds in many ways. Yes, you can blame an earthquake on Elvis.

Music isn't the only source of audible energy frequencies that are causing the gradual destruction of Nature. All intentionally-organized sound waves are to blame. I don't mean natural sounds like bird songs or people talking, or even loud noises like lawnmowers or jet engines. I'm speaking primarily of intentionally-organized sounds such as music, television programs, movies, video games, and the like. Any time an intentionally-organized sound wave mixes with the Creation Frequency, it alters it in some way. The greater the disruption, the greater the alteration. The result can be, and usually is, catastrophic. That is why Earth has realized a surge in natural disasters over the past few years. The organized sound waves produced by humans have become louder, more chaotic, and more numerous than ever before. As this trend continues on the planet, the number of disasters destroying cities and homes and causing disruption and loss of human lives will also increase. It is likely that Mother H will manipulate Earth's music production to do the final destruction work for her at the end of The Great Plan's countdown. Humanity will, in effect, be responsible for destroying itself.

On a positive note, it is not too late to change. The primary purpose of the Family Triad and the Strong Weet is to convince humans to change their ways and modify their lifestyles to accommodate the Creation Frequency.

If they can do this, then this world would revert to the Eden-like state it has not enjoyed since Atlantis and, before that, Annica. It is also the duty of the Strong Weet to meet together often to help control the conduits for the Creation Frequency that distribute it to every corner of the globe.
MARY: *Din.*
Don't tell me, Mary. I'm getting geared up to ramble.
You are. And you must stop doing what Annie asked you to do there on Hectarus. You need to get back to your office so you can fill the readers in on the discovery of the first few of our Strong Weet.
Are you going to take me back down now?
There are many rooms in the Library of Memory, and you don't have the time to describe all of them. It is far more important to bring the readers up to date. Are you ready?

***

When am I going to be able to do that without your help?
Soon, Din. But now you need to do some work on that computer of yours.
What do you want me to write about?
I believe it's time that you tell the tale of how you came upon the first Strong Weet, Elise.
Your wish is my command.
Swell.
Huh? What did you just say?
Just get to it.

THE DISCOVERY OF
THE FIRST STRONG WEET

Elise was discovered just before I found a publisher for *The Strong Weet Society*. It was a dark and stormy night. Just kidding. Actually, it was a hot and sweaty summer day. I was standing in my kitchen sipping a glass of iced tea when Annie whispered into my ear:

Go into your office and check your email.

As always, I do exactly what my lovely daughter tells me to do, so I went into my office, brought up the email on my computer screen, and there it was, a letter from a publisher. Here's how it all played out after I read that letter.

***

Yes! Annie, this is the publisher that was referred to me by a friend I met on Twitter. All I did was send them an email. I sent about a dozen formal query letters out to a list of publishers last week, but I haven't heard from any of those yet. And here comes this offer from out of the blue.

Everything has happened precisely according to plan, Father. Remember, you wrote in the book that a publisher would find you, not that you would find a publisher. It has happened. Grandma is behind this.

Mother H is behind everything.

She is. And she will work with everyone to ensure the success of our work here. It may start out slowly, but Grandma will make it so at exactly the right moment. Don't forget that everything works together to ensure the conclusion of The Great Plan.

But these publisher folks haven't even read the book yet. They're just asking for the manuscript. What if they read it and hate it?

They won't. They will see the potential in the book.

And they'll be the ones to publish it?

They will.

Okay, now what?

You might want to send them the manuscript.

Oh, yeah. I guess that might help.

And after you've done that, I have another surprise for you.

You're just full of surprises, aren't you?

A Strong Weet is near.

You're kidding. Why can't I feel her? Where is she? Who is she?

You can't feel her because Grandma hasn't activated her DNA yet. When she does that, you will be able to feel her distinctive Weet GLOW.

So, she's not aware of what she really is?

That might be a slow process. All of the Strong Weet will require some conditioning before they can learn what they are and what their relationship is to us. The first step is to activate the additional DNA strands we have been weaving into them over the past several years. Then we will introduce ourselves to them one at a time as they find us. We can continue to incorporate more DNA into them from that point.

How many strands does this one have?

As of this moment, she has six.

So, she needs six more to be complete.

Only four for now. Remember that a human being can only accommodate a maximum of ten DNA strands while they still reside in a human body.

They won't need the last two anyway. Those strands control supernatural abilities that are impossible while in a body made of water and flesh.

Activation of the sixth strand will enable them to produce specific frequencies required to support The Great Plan, and we will need to instruct them in this process. Activation of the eighth strand will make them fully aware of the distinction between them and humans. That can be a startling revelation and will also require guidance.

Indeed, it will. I remember when I got my eighth strand. What an eye-opener that was.

Your eyes began to open with your sixth. That was when you first learned to distrust human beings. You were a bit ahead of schedule.

Yes, I was. I knew something was different, but I couldn't quite put my finger on it. The only Guides I had through that process were you and your Mother. It would have been a big help if there had been another Hectaran human in my circle of friends to advise me once in a while or clarify things along the way. All I could do was wing it, and every time I made a mistake, you or Mary thumped me on the back of my head and chewed me out.

Elise will be fortunate to have you to help her along the way. Even so, it will not be easy for her. Like you, Elise has experienced JUMPING *into human bodies many times. In this one, however, her early life was chaotic and left her with a great deal of physiological damage to be corrected. We will attempt to do so while working to insert her additional DNA. The healing will be difficult, so her Awakening process will be slower this time than in her past* JUMPS.

That won't be easy on her.

No, it won't. It will be a very stressful time. Her emotions will play havoc with her conscious mind, but I believe she will soon have them under control. The important thing is that her sixth strand is active, and she can now produce the necessary frequencies. She has gained complete control of her Hum. She knows the feeling of what the Hum does inside of her and uses it well for this purpose, but she is not aware of its true intent and power.

Elise's Hum is a tool for manipulating and fine-tuning the Creation Frequency and advancing The Great Plan. It will be up to you to watch when and how she uses it. Go slowly and let her show you what she knows of herself at first.

Annie, we should explain what Elise's Hum is.

Right. This Strong Weet received a special and unique vibrational gift at the time of her birth on Hectarus. Humans think of a "hum" as a sound emanating through closed lips — a kind of singing with one's mouth closed. Elise's Hum, while similar in production, is entirely different and carries tremendous power. Earth consists of only a few elements, and Elise's Hum strengthens them and binds them together. The Hum is also essential to Grandma's work down here, and only Elise can produce it.

Is Elise aware of all this? These facts are true, and her Hum is enormously important, but I don't want to overwhelm her with information about her powers. It will be hard enough for her to let go of her past and integrate into the present. I think she's going to have a difficult time trusting me — or anyone else, for that matter. It's amazing how garbage from the past can entrap the human mind.

She is frustrated because she feels powerful, but she has been deeply scarred by so many people in her Earthly life. Like all our Hectaran family down here, she is precious to us. She will come to remember the truth about her Hum more quickly than you may expect. Be patient with her, and don't take it personally when she behaves horribly toward you from time to time. The next few years might not be pretty. She needs compassion, especially from you.

So, what now? I'll send the manuscript off to the publishers, but then what? And when do I meet this Strong Weet?

The publishers will read the manuscript, and then they

will offer you a contract. It will take about five months to edit the Diary and place it on the market.

Five months? Jeez. I'll be an old man by then.

Don't be so dramatic. The months will go by quickly, and, believe me, you will have your hands full. You won't even notice the time passing.

You mean I'll be working on *Volume Two* of the *Diary*?

You will, and you will be spending much time and energy locating the Strong Weet to Awaken them to their true nature. That will not be easy.

How hard can it be?

You will see. It begins now. A Weet is near.

What do you mean? Where?

Weren't you going to mow your lawn today?

I was.

Then you'd better get to it.

I'm not sure it really needs it. I was looking at it this morning, and the grass isn't nearly as long as I thought. In fact, I think it's too short for the mower to do much good.

Just go mow the lawn, Daddy. I have to leave anyway. It will give you something to do to keep you out of trouble.

Ha.

Ha, indeed.

***

I own two houses right next to each other. I live in one, and my Earth mother lived in the other one until she needed to be placed in a rest home a couple of years ago. I hate the way that sounds — "placed in." Since she's been away, I have not found a renter for her house — not that I've been trying very hard. Since I Awakened to the knowledge of who I am and of what lies beneath this land, I'm not so sure I want anyone who does not belong here to occupy my mother's house. It is a bit surprising, though, that the little effort I've put into the search has not produced a renter. The economy isn't so hot right now, and a nice little place at a reasonable rent like this one should have been snatched up pretty fast. Maybe this is Annie's doing. I don't think she's too keen on having what she calls "civilians" living on Annica.

At any rate, the house next door is vacant; the walls are newly painted; the floors have been cleaned and sanitized—the whole bit. It is in pristine condition, as are the lawns that I manicure with my riding mower at least once every two weeks after it rains. Summertime here in the Midwest tends to produce rain in abundance, as it did last week. I expected to find some pretty tall grass waiting for me, but when I checked it out earlier this morning, the lawn did not need mowing. But Annie insisted that I mow it, so off I went to the barn. I gassed up the riding mower and drove it over to my mother's front lawn, where the short grass lay before me, basking in the warm sun. I thought then that it was odd that the grass was still short after that rain. I actually considered the possibility that the Faeries might have played a trick on me and mowed the lawn while I was asleep.

Then I saw her—a woman I didn't recognize off in the distance, was busy mowing the nearest neighbor's lawn with a push mower. She had two small children with her, a boy and a girl, who played as she pushed the heavy mower around with apparent ease.

I knew the man who lived in that house, and I was familiar with the people he associated with regularly, but this woman with the children was not one I had seen before. Every time I was about to catch a glimpse of her face, she moved behind a tree or a bush so that I couldn't. At one point, she pushed the mower around the house and disappeared behind it.

For some reason, losing sight of her caused me to panic. My heart pounded. Annie had said that a Weet was near. Could this be her? My anticipation increased as I heard the mower clacking around the neighbor's backyard. I thought, *Is this one of the Strong Weet? God, what if it is? What do I do now? How do I meet her? Where is she? What's she doing back there?*

Finally, I saw the front of the mower come up over the rise of the side yard. I held my breath as the mower handle followed it, and then the hands and the arms of the woman. What the heck was going on? Why did I come out to mow a lawn that didn't need cutting in the first place, and why was I reacting like this? Why was I feeling so weak and drained of energy?

Then her face appeared. She was very pretty. She looked familiar, but I couldn't quite place where — or even if — I had seen her before. One thing was certain — the GLOW that flowed from this woman's mortal frame was unmistakable. It set her apart from all other humans I had known in this life. Its color was brilliant gold, and rays shooting out in all directions captured the sunlight and filled the whole neighborhood with so much glory that not a single person who happened to be within a mile radius was able to move. Silence fell. Even the birds stopped their singing. The world went dead still for just a moment. This was not an ordinary human being. There could be only one explanation. This woman was a Hectaran inside a human frame. Here was my Weet!

The moment I realized who she was, she looked up, and our eyes met. The enormous depth of her soul became evident in that one split second. I was overcome by that feeling that all Hectarans get when they unexpectedly meet one of their own kind. I saw that she, too, was affected by the encounter. She gave me a questioning, puzzled look, but despite her perplexity, she smiled. This was a special moment. A discovery. A finding. Two eternal spirits who had perhaps known each other back on Hectarus, but whose memories had been shaken from them when their Spirits were stuffed into these mortal human containers.

I can't remember the exact words of the conversation we had out on the lawn. All I can remember is the woman walking toward me. When she had covered the distance between us stood before me, she simply said, "Hello, I am Elise."

I had the strong urge to answer her greeting by coming back with, "Hello, I am Din," using the name by which I am known on Hectarus. I didn't. I could tell by looking at her that she had not yet Awakened to her true identity. "Hello," I stuttered. "I'm DH."

From that point forward, my memory is befuddled, as if the words of our conversation had been purposely erased. I remember her face, though. I'd been reading a book about Gauguin, and the images of Tahiti that filled my mind led me to recognize the island influence in her face—olive skin, large almond eyes, broad nose, generous mouth. I could see her sitting for a painting in a grove of coconut palms. She indeed was quite lovely.

I didn't know what to say to her. I felt shy and perhaps a bit afraid of speaking to this stranger who, along with the other Strong Weet I had yet to meet, was about to become a significant part of my life. I actually bit my tongue and could taste the warm blood inside my mouth. I pulled out a piece of spearmint gum and began chewing so that Elise wouldn't see the blood on my teeth. Our conversation was pretty mundane and ended with a plan for me to call Elise soon and arrange for her to visit the Gardens that cover the land, Annica, the center of which is now the activated Altar of Annica situated over the site of the Temple of the ancient and buried empire of Annica.

Elise Visits the Annican Gardens

Elise came by today. She told me she had dropped her kids off at soccer practice and had to pick them up in two hours. I was thrilled to have any time with her at all, but with only two hours, I had to move fast so that we could form the connection between us that would lead her to realize that she is a part of the Strong Weet circle. Her Awakening and the gathering and activation of her power as a Strong Weet depended mainly on how much time we could spend together. When Weet are apart, their frequencies weaken. If Weet have connections through past life relationships, family, or other close associations, separation can cause illness or even death. I offered her a glass of tea even though I could see that she had a quart-sized container filled with some strange dark brew of her own.

"It's a mixture of slippery elm, burdock root, rhubarb, and red raspberry leaves," she said, then swallowed a generous gulp. "I don't go anywhere without my tea, but I will take a glass of what you have."

I handed it to her as we walked out the kitchen door and down the path leading to Annica Gardens.

"I have a dear friend named Sit, and she is the one who built all of these Gardens," I told Elise as she gazed about the incredible expanse. "I don't know much about plants in particular, so I was really happy when Sit chose to do this. She's a master when it comes to the green world."

"It's exquisite. I feel like I've been here before," Elise said, almost as if she was talking to herself. I don't think she intended for me to hear her statement. I was curious, but I didn't question her about it.

"Sit is obviously hugely gifted with a connection to

Flower Spirits. Just look at these arrangements." Elise glowed with delight and smiles as she spoke. "She's followed a perfect geometrical symmetry throughout this whole garden. Each flower family is planted in harmony with the daily measure of sunlight given to this land. Do you see your big tree over there? I can tell that she studied this back space long and deeply before she made any move. What a graceful eye she has. How long have you been friends with her?"

Elise walked slowly and carefully, scanning the whole of the many and varied Gardens with her eyes.

"Oh, for a very long time. Sit is one of the most serious members of the paranormal investigation team I began eons ago. She has been deeply involved with the investigations. She is not only a masterful gardener but has amazing technical skills as well. She handles all the equipment we use in our investigations and always holds a powerful and quiet presence in our walks. We collected a lot of the evidence we did because of her nature and Spirit. Her powers are quite unique, and she is very humble about them. We have researched and visited dozens of places around here and have become good friends over the years."

"The way Sit planted these beauties so meticulously is truly unique. I love how she placed Purple Clematis so that it would adorn the statue of the woman back there. Purple is by far my most cherished and favorite color," Elise said as she turned her back to me and squatted down in front of the statue of Mother H.

I let her continue without interruption.

"You know, it is obvious to me that Sit is something magical. I have never met her and have no idea what she looks like, but I can see her in these Gardens. She must be quite brilliant. Tell me more about her, DH."

"Well, she's a scientist and works long hours in a laboratory at the university conducting biological studies. She's highly respected and works closely with some big-name researchers. She has a passion for biology and the curiosity of a cat. I think she's read every book on the planet about plants and animals, but you won't ever find her tooting her own horn. In fact, you'd be hard-pressed to get her to talk about herself or her achievements at all. Her presence exudes grace and strength. I know her well, but there is also a deep mystery about her that I think only the plants are privy to."

I had a flashback about Sit at that moment, and I related it to Elise.

"One time, I came out here while she was planting those roses around the center of the main Altar Garden. At the time, I had a special rock sitting there, and she seemed to be communing with it, talking with it just like you and I are speaking now. She would say something, then wait and listen, smile, and quietly continue her side of the conversation. She handled those roses like they were the baby Jesus as she planted them. I never asked her about that, but I have always appreciated the beautiful radiance she exuded in her creation of these Gardens. It was almost as if she had a direct calling to be the one to build all of this. Mary and Annie had told me that Sit was indeed "called" to be the keeper of the Annican Altar and the gardens around it. Back home on Hectarus, before she came to Earth, she was the Keeper of the Temple Grounds. There was more about Sit that Elise would need to learn but now was not the time.

"Yes, I know this is true. Well, I do hope to have the honor of meeting Sit sometime in the future. What an angel she must be."

I thought then that their meeting would be soon.

Elise went past one of the water features on the path on our way back to the house. She had told me at our first meeting that she was a musician, and I could almost feel her drinking in the sound of the bubbling water as if the bursting bubbles were serenading her very presence. She giggled a little bit and then proceeded over to the giant Linden tree at the northwest side of the Celtic Garden, the tree under which I recorded *Volume One* of this *Diary*.

Neither of us spoke as she raised her arms and placed both hands high on the tree's trunk, palms flat on the rough bark, thumbs and index fingers of both hands touching, making a tear or a raindrop shape in between. Then she squatted down by the moss on the ground, dancing her fingers across the velvety green.

"I feel the Faeries strong here," she said without prelude. "One must take care where there is moss because the Faeries use it to sleep on." She stroked the moss as if it were the skin of a friend who had just popped in to be with her.

Elise stood up slowly. I stayed my distance and watched. I dared not invade any memory she might be recalling. I wanted this to be all her own.

She took her time at the spot where the Appen ceremony had taken place. She circled the small space and seemed particularly interested in the bricked area that set it apart. She said nothing and moved softly, weightlessly, never once turning up the smallest grain of sand beneath her feet.

The sun shone down on her tanned shoulders. I've never seen human flesh glisten with such intensity. She shone with a bright aura arising from her neck and shoulders. I knew that it was more than a mere aura. It was her GLOW, her inner essence fighting to escape the physical body she had chosen to place herself in just before she

JUMPED into this world.

She followed the garden walkway past the roses and suddenly became chatty.

"I adore flowers of every kind. When I was a child, my father planted all sorts of roses. I would use their buds and branches as make-believe microphones. I would sing a new song for each little rose, and each song became that rose's own personal song until the rose passed from this world."

Elise approached the zinnias and said, "I hope you come over to see my garden's zinnias. This year they stand over six feet tall. I included sunflowers with the ones near the waterfall. I love zinnias because they are like little rainbows who come up so easily, but I love sunflowers more because—"

I held my breath, waiting to hear, but she was distracted by the statue of Mother H on the northeast side of the Altar Garden. Did she know about Annie and her love for sunflowers? Was she about to tell me something that would tell me that she was Awakening to any of this? I wasn't about to ask her to complete her thought, though, because I wanted to see what came next.

She became quiet again as she approached Mother H's statue. I waited for a moment before speaking to her. "That's the Mother of Humankind. I was born on a Monday—Mother H's day—so she is especially important to me. Do you know of her?"

"Yes, she is associated with the moon. People are generally confused about her and don't know what to call her. They've given her many names over the centuries, but I don't think any of them were given to her by herself. Somehow, I have that knowledge inside me, but I don't know much more about her. I am willing to learn, though."

I stood next to Elise. All I could do, or rather all that Mother H would permit me to do, was smile.

"Oh, the time! I have to pick my kids up at noon." Her blissful expression changed as her thoughts suddenly returned to the mundane world.

"But you've only seen the Altar Garden and the Celtic Garden," I told her. "There's also the Faerie Garden, the Garden of Contemplation, the Fruit Garden, Mother's Garden, the Golden Forest Garden, the St. Francis Garden, The Garden of the Virgin Mary …"

She gave one last wistful look around the Garden then sighed, "This place is miraculous."

"Yes, it is," I agreed.

"I wish I didn't have to leave yet, but the kids … The soccer coach gets a bit pissy if I'm late."

She doesn't remember that there is no time where we are from. Then she surprised me.

"You know, I like infinity," she said blithely. "Yes, I have to rush off to pick up the kids because I agreed to believe in the way time works here, and I really am the most punctual person you will ever know. But I will share a secret with you, DH. Linear time is a lie, but everybody believes in it. It's a tool used by those who think they are in control to keep everyone else in line. They say, 'You're born, you go school, you get your degree or trade so you can pay your bills, but watch out, you're bound to get sick as you grow older, so you'd better have that insurance. And don't forget Social Security because when you're too old to keep working as the cog you are, you'll need our pennies to fall back on. Oh, yeah, then all your left-over bills will go to your family when you die.' This is what our fear culture has everyone believing, and it's a big lie."

I was stunned. She had spouted this all out rapid-fire, but, judging from her expression, she may as well have been reading the weather report. She blinked, smiled, then took another huge gulp of tea.

"Can we go inside the house before you leave? I have some things I'd like to give you if you want them." I only had a few minutes left with her, and I wanted to make the most of them.

"Of course. Will you give me a hint? I love surprises, but I also like guessing what they could be." She turned to face the Gardens and made a quick half-bow, half curtsey. She did it in a way that made me think I wasn't supposed to see—but I did.

While we walked back along the paths to the house, I told her, "This is your hint: they come from all over the world, and I know that you will use them well in the healing work that you do." She'd told me during our first meeting that she took part in a weekly healing session. It's probably no coincidence that it is the same one that I was involved in a few years ago. I dropped out when my Awakening led me to know that the healing sessions are a complete fraud—but I didn't tell her that. She would be attending one of those sessions this evening.

"I know you'll love some of the gifts, but you may not have any use for all of them."

When we got back to the house, I went into my office to get a bag filled with small stones. I had collected many of them during my travels, and friends from all over the world had sent nearly as many to me. I returned to the living room to find Elise sitting in the center of the couch, grinning with excitement and anticipation. She reminded me of a little girl getting ready to open a birthday present.

I sat down next to her and opened up the cloth pouch. Each stone was in a little plastic bag along with a note stating where and when the stone was found and if the stone had been a gift, who found it. I pulled them out one by one, adding as much drama to the moment as I could, and watched her eyes grow wider as I explained the origin of each stone.

"This one is from my ancestral home in Scotland. It comes from the beach on Loch Laggan that caresses the land directly in front of what once was the castle of the MacPhersons, my family clan."

She held out her hands to take it, her right palm under her left hand as if she were accepting the Eucharist at a Catholic Mass. She breathed a soft, "Oh," brought the grey stone to her chest, and held it next to her heart before carefully — almost reverently — setting it on the coffee table in front of us.

One by one, I gave her the piece of the pyramid of Giza from Egypt, a stone from Machu Picchu, one from Stonehenge, another from Petra, the fabulous red rock city in the Middle East, and a unique stone from Jerusalem's Wailing Wall — a small stone with a tiny hole all the way through it. Elise went through the same motions each time, letting silent tears fall as she blessed each rock.

I reached the bottom of the bag and paused. "If you don't want this last one, I'll understand. It's got a different energy."

Elise looked at the note that accompanied the rough, gray rock. It read, "From Adolf Hitler's Wolf's Lair."

"Oh, my Goodness. The combination of all this is unreal, DH. Of course, I want all of these — especially this last one. I already know how I will use it for healing. These gifts hold more meaning for me than anything I have ever received. I really can't find words to express my gratitude for this gift."

Her smile was all I needed.

"Take the stones to that healing session you're going to tonight and let me know what happens with any of them."

"Of course I will. And I'm really sorry I have to leave so soon, but I'll email you as soon as I get back to the computers at the library. I wish I had my own computer, but I just can't afford it." She picked up her purse and the bag of stones and reluctantly stood to leave.

"Yes," I said as we walked together to the front door. "A computer with internet at home would make communication easier. I have a feeling we're going to be seeing a lot of each other." I smiled with the knowledge of the truth of that statement.

"I know someone who might be able to help me out with that, DH. I will get to work on that ASAP."

"Great. Enjoy the stones, and don't be a stranger to this place."

"I won't. Thank you so much for all you have given me." She smiled, and I hugged her, planting a kiss on the crown of her head.

***

It's difficult to put into words what Elise's visit meant to me. A Strong Weet has appeared, just as Annie said she would. Now for the process of Elise's Awakening. Most of it is her responsibility and requires her to make the right decisions in her life and pay close attention to all of the information Annie and I give her. The goal is to trigger the identity memories coded into our DNA every time we JUMP into a new body. Lack of information can conceal identity memories and their revelation is slowed by wrong decisions made in our early Earth lives before our Awakening begins. I know very little about Elise's first thirty-three years at this writing, so it's difficult to estimate the time it will take for her to Awaken fully. It took me several years, and I was working with a body that had suffered only minor damage from wrong decisions.

My problem, as evidenced in *Volume One* of the *Diary*, was my own hardheadedness and impatience. Hopefully, Elise will have to contend with neither of those.

The most important thing that I can do for Elise is to help her to Awaken at least to the point where she has the desire to trust me and to learn from me. All of the Strong Weet and the Secondary Weet will undergo a similar process which may well be harder on me than it is on them. These Weet will all have had different backgrounds and experiences and will have different ways of looking at this world. It will not be to bring them around to where they can see beyond surface appearances or to focus on the primary task of repairing the Creation Frequency to save this planet from destruction. The biggest problem I will likely encounter in the Weet will be inflated or misdirected ego. That and, possibly, even instability of mind.

All DNA, be it human, other Earth species, or Hectaran, is subject to damage over time and generations. There is no telling just what kind of damage or how much has occurred over multiple lifetimes of exposure to things such as drugs, alcohol, negative emotions, poor diet, and bad habits. Also, false information greatly compounds the effects of such damage. There is always an abundance of spurious knowledge, and the Weet seem to be particularly susceptible to it, especially in their unawakened state. Annie has told me that a few of the unawakened Weet of this generation have been led astray by unscrupulous fraudsters claiming to offer spiritual guidance of one persuasion or another. The risk to Elise is even greater because of her intense GLOW. Also, because her nature and looks are appealing, men of all types are drawn to her, often with bad intentions. Mother and Annie have already been forced to "remove" a few of those men from Elise's path. What Elise must learn quickly is that the men are harmful to her GLOW. Their presence can distort it, make her Hum ineffective, and even harm her physical health.

All of these factors could affect the stability of the Weet soon to enter our little fold. I will have to deal with what will be a long and challenging task. Mental instability, if present, will not affect the Weet's ability to use their Hectaran frequency to help realign the Creation Frequency. We may even find that since the conscious human mind is far less advanced than the Hectaran mind, a little instability might be a good thing.

***

Much has happened since my introduction to Elise. In addition to the publication of *Volume One* of the *Diary*, Elise moved into the house left vacant by my mother. She and her children needed a place to stay, and I had the house ready for her. What a wonderful convenience it is. It's much easier for me to instruct and guide Elise as she continues to Awaken. The process is moving along well despite a few glitches. She's even progressing faster than I did, I might add. Of course, her DNA is still not complete. She's up to seven strands now and is working on her eighth, but that is one of the more difficult strands to insert into a human system.

It has not been easy for Elise to get to where she is today. There have been many ups and downs and more than a few moments of trauma, and there will be more. She has made incredible progress, however, and recognizes her true identity as a Strong Weet. She has the growing sense that she might be something even more. What that is must remain a mystery for now. She is not yet ready to handle that information. That knowledge will Awaken in her naturally at the proper time. Until then, we have much to do, and she has much more to learn.

There have been some extreme emotional meltdowns since Elise moved in next door. It has not been easy for her to transform her human body into that of a Hectaran. That process causes changes to her physical human body along with increasing awareness of certain realities. For instance, she has become aware that nearly everything she was taught while growing up as a human means nothing. She now knows that many people she once thought of as friends are not just insincere in their friendship toward her, but stand in opposition to everything Elise has learned to be truth. One of the perks—some might say curses—of being decended from a Hectaran Being is that truth is easily discernible in every situation. It can be read on a face and easily deciphered by observing the actions of others. In our case, we have the added advantage of constantly receiving into our minds a stream of truth and information from our family of Higher Beings. No one can hide their true motives from us. They can say one thing with their lips, but immediately Annie, Mary, or even Mother H will speak to our minds the truth of their intentions. Several of Elise's friends have been unmasked in this way. It was hard for her at first to accept that people she once trusted and thought she loved were actually liars and manipulators. The infusion of the seventh strand of DNA imparts the ability to discern such things and deal with them unemotionally, a skill that Elise is quickly fine-tuning. She is also learning how to communicate with the Family more clearly and efficiently.

Speaking of family, I'd like to clarify some of the Hectaran Family relationships concerning Earth humans and Hectarans. All of the Strong Weet and Secondary Weet are part of the Family, including Din (me), Mary, Annie, and Mother H, whom they are allowed to call "Mother." Mother H is every Hectaran's Mother and, as

Family members with strong Hectaran lineage, the twenty-four Strong and Secondary Weet should not hesitate to acknowledge that. While the numerous Support Weet maintain a spiritual connection to the Hectaran Family, their physical relationship to the Founders is distant at best. It is disrespectful for them to refer to Mother H as Mother. Throughout their history, the humans of Earth have used their impression of Mother H, whom they also know as Mother Nature, as the model for the numerous imaginary deities in the female form set up to and worshiped in all the cultures of that planet. Even today, there are multitudes of humans who consider themselves the sons and daughters of this or that goddess or even Mother, Herself. That is not the case and is merely wishful thinking on their part.

One last distinction is that the Strong and Secondary Weet are not a part of the Family Triad. The Family Triad consists only of the three Created Beings, Mary, Din, and Annie, and is at the highest level of communication between Hectarus and Earth. The Triad's primary duties are to oversee the maintenance and function of the Creation Frequency on Earth and direct the implementation of The Great Plan when the time comes. That may sound simple, but it involves the identification, Awakening, and training of the Strong and Secondary Weet and the recruitment and training of the Support Weet. To put it in military terms, The Family Triad are the generals, the Strong Weet are the higher-ranking officers, The Secondary Weet are the lower-ranking officers, and the Support Weet are the enlisted personnel.

When Elise first received mental communication from Annie, it brought tears to her eyes. Now, talking with Annie is an everyday thing for her. When Mother H began to make herself known, Elise was a little frightened by the power she felt in that connection. Now, though, she readily goes to Mother H with matters that concern her.

Mother H and Annie started revealing themselves to Elise when she received her first infusion of Hectaran DNA. Human DNA alone cannot support clear, two-way communication between Earth humans and Hectarans, so Elise had only a vague awareness of their presence. To hasten and guide her awaking, Mother and Annie would do things like rearranging the furniture in Elise's house just enough so that she would notice. They also took great delight in distributing small rubber ducks from the flotilla the children kept in the bathtub to various unlikely spots all around the house. It wasn't unusual for Elise to open the refrigerator and find one of those little yellow duckies smiling out at her.

When Elise bought some magnetic alphabet letters and placed them on the refrigerator door for her children to practice making words, Mother H and Annie used them to leave personal messages for Elise to find. They arranged the letters into complete sentences with words that clearly indicated that the activity was neither random nor a prank by the children. The messages were usually lighthearted, but sometimes their meaning was pointed. Mother H and Annie wanted Elise to know beyond any doubt that they were not only with her, but they also experienced everything that she experienced. They also wanted her to know that they were just a breath away. It was in these ways that they made their Spirit Energy known and comfortable to Elise.

When Elise moved in next door six months ago, I gave her a copy of *Volume One*. She read through it quickly and continues to refer to it as her Awakening, or Inter-fusion as she calls it, progresses. Elise has been through and overcome a great deal on her personal journey and sharing her thoughts would be helpful to her and of value to those who read them. I will save that for later, though. These months have been eventful, and Annie wants me to have Elise relate events from her point of view.

Excerpts from Elise's Diary

Din asked me to write of my experiences in these past couple of months and maybe even all the things I experienced before moving in here. I will give it a go because I need clarity on so much, and writing has always been one of the most potent medicines I know. He even said that this might go into *Volume Two* of the series he is working on. Something extraordinary and powerfully wonderful is happening. I wish to God I knew what it was all about. I do know that powerful and mysterious feelings of a sort of homecoming began to consume me as I was reading *Volume One* of *Mary's Diary*. Compelling and strange feelings of some kind of homecoming came over me. My head felt as if it were cracking open to let in the true knowledge of who I am. It's all so beautiful, but I feel like I have amnesia. It angers me to feel so stuck.

Plus, how totally weird and ironic is it that my personal journal will soon be available to the world? Oh well, I have nothing to hide, so here goes.

Crazy. I am crazy. No, Elise is crazy, fully and completely, and it is such a pain in the fanny dealing with her. Yes, I am talking about myself in the third person because "Elise" is not who I AM. But who, really, am I? I walk around in this body — this costume of flesh — that I inhabit only for this lifetime and deal with a head full of lies. That part is clear. It is this whole process of exorcism I am immersed in that drives me crazy. Yes, exorcism, because that is what it takes to detach, not from some dark demon, but from my own ego. The more I realize how securely my belief in and attachment to my identity and my self-centered thoughts about myself and the world have imprisoned me, the more my ego disgusts me. I can't annihilate my ego, however, because then I wouldn't be here, doing this work for God, THE ALL — I like that Name for God. It describes Who He truly is, ALL. Even so, I'm not sure exactly what my work is to be.

There is great purpose in having met Din, and I love it, even though so much remains a mystery. I feel a glimmer inside me now all the time, and I know that I am something so much greater than my already creative and poetic mind can imagine. I know that I am a spirit, but the question still eats at me: *Who* am I, and why don't I remember? Bits and pieces pop into my head now and then, but never the complete picture.

My conversations with Din are a big help. Since that first day in the garden, our interactions have been like a crystal lens for me. Everything we talk about sends a thrilling rush of energy through my spine. I know it sounds strange, but I am at home when I am in his presence.

I wish I could understand why. I guess I should be content just to feel so good, but the Lord knows I have always been impatient. I go from ordinary awareness to experiences of cosmic flying at the drop of a hat. All these supernatural teases need to become more constant for me to understand any of them.

Shh, Elise. Just remember that the Interfusion needs time to do the work inside of you.

Right. Interfusion. Yes, I like the word. I think it is the same as the word "Awakening" that Din uses in *Volume One*, but I believe Interfusion better describes what has been happening to me. It is getting stronger now.

Long before I moved in to this lovely house here on Annica — it's been six months now — soon after the birth of my first child, I began to experience surges of energy whoosh through my body. I'd be cooking dinner or nursing the baby, then suddenly have to hold on to something — not easy to do with a baby in my arms — while a kind of cosmic rush catapulted through my flesh and blasted through my head. It seemed at first that the whooshes caused me to lose consciousness. The light of the energy was so intense that all I was aware of was this mega-force exploding across my vision. These episodes would last about ten seconds, and then I would regain awareness and see myself right where I started, wherever I'd been in my house. I had no idea then of what was going on. I tried to rationalize the situation by telling myself that I wasn't eating enough protein — after all, breastfeeding mothers need to consume an extra 1,500 to 2,000 calories per day — but the whooshes continued well beyond the seven years I nursed my two children.

During this time, I also began to question everything about my life and the people in it. Soon, nothing about any of it felt right, and I began to doubt the sincerity of everyone I knew. The births of my two blessed children in my own home and mothering were the only things that felt right and true. These were pure and natural for me.

I was changing into something new but also somehow old and familiar. I was deeply confused on some days, and I felt trapped without knowing why. Even so, I knew that something big was happening to me that I had to ease into with great care.

I have always been a journaler, poet, and songwriter/ singer, so it was natural for me to take refuge in my voice, paper, and pen. Everything I felt and thought poured out of me onto the pages of my diaries. When I read them now, I laugh at my observations of the beginnings of my Awakening, or Interfusion as I call this strange and wonderful process of letting go of lies and attachments and the revelation of my *real* Being. Din can attest to how very impatient I have been for the past six months, but I am willing to challenge myself and be more patient. Nonetheless, I am far enough along in the process to have acquired some abilities that are nothing like those of any other human, that's for sure.

ELISE AND THE CHERRY TREE

Elise is so utterly strange and yet familiar. I know who she is, and her behavior and speech indicate that she knows she is not typical of this culture, this society, and this world. I hesitate to confront her directly about her true nature, as she has been living here on Annica for only a few months. Also, I have instructions not to feed her any information unless directed by Mother H or Annie, so I must be patient. I know how delicate the Awakening process can be. I don't want to scare her off, but I am concerned that the voice of her own strongly-attached ego might do just that. What to do?

Go outside now and watch her. You will know more about how far along she is in her Awareness by watching her right now.

Annie, am I glad to see you. I have some questions I want to run by you about our little Weet living here on Annica.

I said go!

But, Annie—

You need to witness what that little Weet is doing. It will give you much to think about.

Oh, all right. This better be good.

***

There are several small barns and sheds on Annica separate from the houses. One of them blocks the view of the section of Gardens behind where Elise lives from the part behind where I live. I walked silently down the stone path that leads around the back of the barn to where the two sections come together. I stopped when I heard the soft murmur of Elise's voice, but Annie practically made my muscles freeze.

Listen!

Okay, okay. This is making me feel like a Peeping Tom, but I get it.

As I listen, Elise's murmurs resolved into words. *"Padre Dios, te doy mi vida."*

Annie, I don't understand Spanish. What did Elise just say? How am I supposed to get that?

Then Elise began singing. The melody was haunting, and the words were not English but sounded something like Spanish. She laughed between her breaths of song while I stood impatiently at the edge of the barn and wondered what the heck she was doing out there in the Gardens.

Again, she spoke, *"Padre Dios, te doy mi vida."*

This time, I sensed that she was moving. I was getting frustrated with only hearing, so I took another step forward to peek through the hedge hiding me.

Elise was facing east, which meant that her back was toward me and she couldn't see me. She was seated on the ground in front of the Cherry tree that had not born any fruit since I planted it a few years ago. She appeared to be praying with her hands raised high over her head.

She remained unmoving, with her hands over her head, for at least five minutes. *"Padre Dios, te doy mi vida!* Father God, I give my life to you."

She finally stood and turned to face south. I pulled back so I would not disturb her, or more importantly, so she wouldn't see me. Is Elise farther along than I thought? She's just standing, looking up at the sky. Now she's just walking away.

Annie? Are you still here?

Thirty Minutes Later

I feel a little better now that I've had some tea and thought some about what I saw. What had Elise been saying? She was talking to God. She was telling God that she is giving her life to Him. I wonder if He was talking back to her. Was He answering Elise?

I need to find the right moment to speak with Elise about it. That will come.

Elise's Diary Continues

There is something so completely perfect and beautiful about living here in this new house near Din's. There are frequencies here on this land that make me feel like I never want to leave. I was talking to God recently out in the Gardens. I sensed for the first time that God and Mother were right here — right inside me. I believe I know God at least as much as anyone can know the Great Mystery that is God. But Mother, there is so much about you, Mother, that I do not know. I always thought that my down-deep knowing of the Earth gave me knowledge of exactly Who You are. I know, though, that there is so much more. I need to speak with Din about all of this. I know he can help me understand some things. Maybe help jump-start some connections in this brain of mine.

When I was out in the Gardens earlier facing that sweet little Cherry tree, strange swirls and swooshes filled the air around my raised arms. It was exhilarating. I felt watched but protected, like a Presence more immense than even I can dream of cradled me as I stood there in the Garden.

I feel so frustrated because even though I know this land where I now reside, I can't quite recall *how* I came to know it. I hate this amnesia I live with, and right now, I'm really ticked off and confused about it. I need to let go of these feelings and emotions because all they have ever brought me are destruction and pain. Phew! Yep, at least it's getting easier to free myself of my feelings. What lies have filled this head of mine all of my life.

The good news is that a wealth of weird and wonderful gifts has been coming to me lately. At first, it was a bit troubling because I encountered things that seemed to have nothing to do with my life.

One of these fantastic gifts has been the ability to see clearly and in detail the lives of two women who live in this town. They feel very familiar to me, but I am still trying to figure out why I know details of their lives. I guess God is behind it. He has made me into a voyeur of sorts, and I am supposed to tell what I know about both of them.

First, though, I need to talk with Din about Mother and all this stuff running through me. I need this right now.

Truth is Revealed to Elise

I closed my journal and looked up to see Din strolling down the red brick pathway. Synchronicity is very cool. His appearance at the moment I needed to talk with him tells me something. There is no such thing as coincidence.

"What's up?" he said.

"Needing to talk with you, that's what's up. I hate this not knowing stuff. Can you tell me something about myself? God, that sounds so pitiful. So much I already know in my blood and bones, but there is this something that I cannot name that I am desperate to embrace. I do this 'praise thing' every month to honor God and Mother, the Spirit of Earth, Whom I've come to love and respect over the years. Now, though, I'm beginning to wonder if I even really know who Mother is at all. I don't know what's going on." I dug my hands down into the dirt as far as they would go.

The sound of the spring peepers filled the air as I waited in the warm sun for Din to speak.

"Are you ready for this, Elise?"

"As ready as I'll ever be. Bring it on."

"You are one of the ten Strong Weet that I mentioned in *Volume One* of *Mary's Diary*. You are from Hectarus, and you are far more powerful than you give yourself credit for or that you are even capable of knowing right now. How's that for clarity?"

"Well, honestly, that's something I've suspected for a while, but I've not been able to acknowledge it fully yet. It's really kind of freaky to read about oneself in a published book, you know?"

Suddenly, the truth hits me. "Oh, my God. Mother, Mother, Mother! Of course, my sweet Mother! It's been you all along. Mother of Humankind! Mother H! Okay, this is good. This is better. For a long time, I have been unsure about the connection between God and Mother, but now it all makes sense. You know what I mean?"

"Yes, I do, Elise," Din said. The look on his face told me that he knew so much more.

I laid back on the soft Earth. "Now that we have that out of the way, I need to be alone so that I can get rid of this head of mine," I said. "It's caused enough damage already in this lifetime, and I'm going to need to go places I haven't been to before, inside, and beyond if you get my drift. This could take a while, Din."

"Yup, I gotcha. You want me to get lost, but just be aware that you will never be able to go so far away that I can't find you. I want you to come and talk to me about anything, okay? I know you're aware that you are dealing with the remnants of the mind of Elise as they conflict with the mind of your true spirit. There is more for you to embrace and still more that you must let go of. I am here to help you with the latter so that you can naturally do the first."

"Okay. Thank you, and I'm sorry."

"You're welcome. Sorry for what?"

"I predict that I will say and do a lot of things that might be hurtful and stupid, so I'm just saying sorry in advance."

"Apology accepted." Din smiled.
I closed my eyes as he walked away.

More Excerpts from Elise's Diary

When it became clear to me that I am the daughter of Mother H, she began to reveal herself to me more frequently. I am still coming to terms with an event that occurred a week ago, and Din has asked me to share that entry from my diary. I know that my true spirit consciousness occupies the human body known as Elise, alongside the human mind of Elise. Even though there is a tug of war going on between us at times, Elise does not mind sharing her life with me. My true Being is a spirit whose name I have not yet recalled, nor has Din told it to me. I have begun to think of Elise in the third person. Elise is the conscious human mind of this body's past, and the name has been retained as the label for this body while I occupy it in this lifetime. I, however, am really—

What a struggle this is for me.

Elise Appeals to Mother H

Mother H was going to do it. She had heeded my fervent prayers. I had been indulging in obnoxious behavior for weeks because I could not bring myself to trust Din's assertion that my past was dead.

Ego rears its ugliness in every possible way, and my attachments to my own very nearly ended my work with Din. I was treating him just like all the other men who had abused me in my short life. Even though I cried when I saw the absurdity of my behavior, I still could not seem to separate myself from a past that haunted me. I prayed to God that He would somehow bring about my release.

Mother H was privy to these prayers and watched over

me as ego prompted me to say or do the most asinine things to Din. I am surprised she didn't annihilate me on the spot.

As with all issues, Mother H must consult with God before making any move. Although Mother H is the conscious, sustaining Energy Being that animates all life in the universe, she still answers to God. She must wait for orders from His Holy Spirit before she can act, and when she does, she has the blessing from His Holy Spirit to proceed at her discretion.

These last two months were painful while I watched Din receive abuse from this tarnished, polluted, and just plain scared world-head of Elise's. There wasn't much I could do. Every negative thought and past memory that I chose to entertain, and the resulting attitudes that I dumped onto Din, interfered with the expression of my true spirit within me. The only thing that saved me was my commitment and determination to work through this in personal silence. It was communion with God through Holy silence that carried me through—that and Din's goodness and infinite patience with me.

Mother H shared with Din that she could not make a move until I admitted that I was trapped and expressed a heartfelt desire to rid myself of the attachment. I guess I finally showed sufficient contrition last night. A brilliant flash of lightning blinded me momentarily. When my vision returned, I found myself lying outside on the Annican Altar, staring up at the storm-laden sky. Then I heard and saw my sweet, precious Mother H.

Mother H Descends in a Purple and Gold Vortex

The rain pelted me, but I continued to lie on my back and watch the steady pulses of lightning ripple across the Blue-Grey evening sky. It is not unusual for me to stay outside during a thunderstorm, so I was not anxious about it, but I would brave the fiercest hurricane to receive a message from Mother H.

What came next filled me with peace and ecstasy.

A Purple and Gold vortex of light appeared in the eastern sky. The funnel began as a tiny point at the center of the vortex. It stretched and reached toward the ground, growing with ferocious beauty as it increased in size. Crystalline sparks of White light spun out from the vortex, and the funnel brightened with Purple and Gold light, illuminating the dark skies. My jaw grew slack, and my mouth filled with rainwater as I watched the workings of Mother H. I knew the display was for me and that I was the only one who could see it.

It takes a lot for Mother to place herself on Earth in recognizable human form and not do any damage in the process. She is so vast that one of her "feet" could easily squash the entire United States were she confronting anyone other than Din or me. Not to worry, though. Mother is more precise than a ballet dancer. She is also in total possession and control of her own will and cannot be summoned or conjured by any human being.

I tell you without a doubt that no human anywhere can tell Mother what to do. No human can order her around like a pet puppy. When Mother chooses to come down here to the surface of this world, it can only mean that she is here for a grave and significant reason, and all humans everywhere should be terrified. Showing herself to me within the Purple of the vortex was, indeed, serious, but it was a personal communing between her and me.

I continued to watch as the irresistible and ominous heavenly thing in the eastern sky grew rapidly larger. Had I seen this a year ago, I would not have understood the otherworldly energy of this force. I would have been sure that it was my end. The Interfusion has been active within me for almost a full year now, and I am far less human now than then, so I was able to watch this rare showing calmly and with great awe.

I began to Hum, as I knew that I was seeing Mother and that her appearance was for me only. This was the moment I had been waiting for. I lay perfectly still, and as I Hummed, the Purple spiral increased in force and deepened with intensity. Suddenly the Gold redirected itself and shot straight into my belly button.

I cannot begin to describe what it was like. Her gift spun me into the Cosmos to visit all the other civilizations out there from one end to the other. With my newly-expanded awareness, I felt like a long-lost traveler finally arriving back at home and greeted the inhabitants as such.

As I sped through the heavens, these words from Mother H went with me:

My daughter, you prayed for intervention to speed the release of the stranglehold your ego had on you. You were sincere, and you felt your heart breaking because you knew that it was never supposed to be that way. I answered your prayer, and now you can complete the work with Din unhindered. The others are out there waiting for you. You know who they are. You must do everything in your power and do it correctly so that you will be ready for them when they appear.

I flew over dozens of stellar colonies populated by Beings devoted to God and in awe of Mother H. I saw the GLOW of the populated star systems from a distance, and as I got closer, I saw details of the inhabitants I felt the purity of peace emanating from these Beings.

I finally saw the stories of Elise's past shoot out of her head, out of her feet, and disappear into nothingness.

Thank God for Mother H's intervention. Thank God that Mother H granted my prayer that I may more rapidly do the work I have been trying to do now for six months with Din.

The Purple of the raging funnel focused on the upper part of my body, and its frequency enveloped my head. That head, formed by my attachment to the human identity, ego, was blown apart by a splendor of cosmic kisses. I felt a peaceful ecstasy as I saw the organic mass implode and explode at the same time.

Then I saw Mother H descend from the vortex. Her Black hair whipped away the clouds, and her piercing eyes consumed my body with her love for me. Not a word passed between us, but she gazed down upon me smiled, and I heard her say:

Now you see, my dear. I have been inside you this whole time. Thank THE ALL that your ego is laid to rest. Your Spirit will be in control from now on.

She leaned down, bringing her face level with mine. She leaned a bit further and sunk her eyes into my forehead. The visitation was complete.

I do not think that Mother H is very far away at all anymore. I hope humanity is ready for this. I believe that I am ready, but I don't think humans know anything at all about what will soon befall them.

Din Introduces the Work of the Color Beings

Elise just told me how Mother H visited her in a physical form. I knew that what she was saying was true because I witnessed it myself — or at least I saw as much as I was allowed.

I was wandering in the Gardens last night, and I became concerned when I saw Elise still outside, sitting on the Annican Altar with that raging storm coming. I wanted to run over there to chew her out and tell her to get her butt back into her house, but Annie stopped me in my tracks. I remember exactly what she said to me:

Let Elise be. Something very, very important is about to happen to her, and you must not interfere. Just relax, and Elise will tell you all about it in good time. She will not be the same.

Well, Annie was right. Elise — it feels strange to call her by that name now — has finally reconnected with her true essence, or Being. This is only the beginning for her, and I am happy to say that I know she can handle it. It has been tough for her, but she has made tremendous progress in just a few short months of living on the Annican land. Detachment is not easy to achieve in a world that tries so hard to keep Spirit Beings stuck in a human mind.

Anyway, in the brief time since Mother H's visitation, Elise, the first of our Strong Weet, has received several important revelations. I have asked her to write of one in particular: Colors and their nature as sentient Beings. These incredible visual creatures dramatically affect everyone and everything on planet Earth, so it is good to know something about them.

In *Volume One* of *Mary's Diary*, Mary hinted at the importance of the presence and placement of Blue in the Annican Temple. That holds for all of the Colors used there.

The Temple floor is an intricately patterned mosaic in which Turquoise tiles create an ocean and sky home for the tiled images of Eagle, Dog, Dolphin, Hummingbird, and a wealth of other spirit animals who once graced Annica but have left the Earth plane forever. The Altar is a solid milky-White block of pure crystalline marble about twelve feet long, three feet wide, and about four feet high. The exact hues and placement of these colors were carefully planned to enhance the energies of communication and creation between Annica and Hectarus. This energetic network woven from the perfectly combined vibrations of the Color Beings supplied sustenance for everything brought forth on this new land by the two Created Beings.

For the time being, the floor and Altar of the Temple lie perfectly preserved beneath the Earth's surface under hundreds of feet of rock and dirt.

ELISE EXPLAINS THE COLOR BEINGS

Colors are not merely pretty variations of light and pigment thrown together for the sake of aesthetic enjoyment. Nor are they simply part of the wondrous handiwork of "Mother Nature," the flora, fauna, and landscape of this planet. They are living Spirit Beings, individually created and ordained by God to serve as conductors, or intermediaries of the Creation Frequency, throughout all universes, especially this one, the home of Mother H's beloved Earth.

I will do my best to describe the nature and function of the Color Beings in all of their hues and shades. I will also be giving them the honor and respect they deserve by capitalizing their names.

Earth is an experiment designed and lovingly watched over by God. The intent was to determine if the inhabitants of a world operating at a slightly lower frequency would maintain their knowledge and adoration of God as well as their connection to Him. The humans of Earth were given Free Will on this new planet created in the image of heaven. They were also given abilities only slightly less extensive and powerful than those possessed by Hectarans. God wanted to see if these beings and their offspring would draw on their connection to Him and use the Creation Frequency to open a new portal through which rejuvenating streams of the Creation Frequency would flow throughout the Milky Way Galaxy and to all the universes.

At first, the three Created Beings were the only ones taught how to work with the colors, as they would be the ones directly responsible for the SEEDING of Earth.

Two of the three Created Beings were sent to this unfinished world to direct the manipulate of sound and light by the Color Beings to complete the work of creation. By speaking the name of a particular Color Being and combining it with a hand gesture, the Created Being could bring forth any desired element or detail of Nature. In that way, all things were created by the wave of a hand and the mention of a color. In other words, under God's direction, Color Beings actively participated in the design of this entire world.

From the nothing which was everything at the very beginning of the Beginning—the infinite and all-encompassing Black from which God created all universes—God commanded forth light. From this single word, "light," the sentient Color Beings were born, each with its own specific designation and purpose in the creation process, unique for every universe.

Mother H assigned each of them to essential tasks, consulting them regarding their thoughts on the planet's formation and structure as an organic body of light.

The Color Beings agreed that they would contribute their energies to the star itself, combining their forces to bring it to life and then rearrange themselves to form the elements we now know to be the original stuff of Earth.

The natural elements that comprise the life forms of Earth are well known to scientists. However, the current arrangements of subatomic and molecular structures were not part of the original design. Silica, for example, is an essential element in the cells of all living creatures. It is the condensed Color Being, White, and is one of the predominant vibratory elements of the building blocks of Nature on Earth. When spoken forth and directed by the Created Beings, White condensed itself into a form based on the pure crystalline code of the primary building block on Hectarus.

Earth exists at a deliberately lower frequency than that of Hectarus. Because of that and Earth's location in the hinterlands of the Milky Way Galaxy, Earth's vibrations required careful fine-tuning. Although Earth's frequencies are different, they must be in harmony with those of Hectarus so that Earth's inhabitants can receive sustaining energy from the home world.

And so, after much consideration and with great care, the Created Beings said, "Green," and miles of forests were born. With the word "Blue," crystal-pure rivers, waterfalls, brooks, streams, and oceans splashed across the landscape. And on it went. For every Color spoken, a specific vocal tone and hand gesture brought forth a unique hue. For thousands of years, the two Created Beings carried out the task of calling forth the sentient Beings of Color to create and maintain the beauty of Nature and all its wonders on this tiny planet. It was here that the story of Adam and Eve living in the Garden of Eden took place, as was so beautifully recorded in the Bible.

These days, some humans profess to be healers, and some of them claim to understand how to use color to promote healing and wellness among their clientele. These assertions are ridiculous and contradict the physical laws of Earth.

Humans can think and feel specific Colors and even invite them to travel up and through their flesh. Nevertheless, the work of opening the human form to a relationship with the Color Beings beyond that basic level is beyond the capabilities of most humans.

There are so-called healers who believe they can control the Color Beings but they are misleading the public. The only *True* healing power is from God.

Color Beings adore the innocent artistic exploration of children, and they do wish that humans could get with it and produce more exciting box sets of crayons.

Color can be talked to and consulted. Children understand this and need to be encouraged to continue in their understanding. Adults need to relearn this. Talking to Colors can open the way to receive healing from God. The practice can also enhance the reception of dreams and intuitions that guide, protect and comfort us.

Color is an excellent guide to nutrition, as well. Those sweet peppers you see in the market are not just Red. They are the Color Being, Red, calling to you in friendship, offering communion with you because you have a urinary tract infection that needs to be addressed, for example. Take your time while admiring a fruit or vegetable, a flower or tree. Color offers an opportunity to reconnect with God.

Color Beings also ask that humans think about how they use speech to summon color.

"I was so mad that I saw Red!"

"I love the Green of the forest. It's so peaceful."

"This breakup has me feeling so Blue."

"I am having a Grey day."

Names are important. How would you feel if you heard your name used as a profanity?

Annie wants to add some thoughts here.

Take care how you use not just God's name but the names of all sentient Beings created from out of the heart of God. Treat them with respect and do not dishonor them. Human beings know little about the eternal life that comes after their physical life ends on this little globe. Please hear and understand these words. It is best not to gamble with what you do not understand. And it would be best if you did not claim to understand what lies beyond when no human being on Earth does.

Thank you, Annie. Color can influence and control a person's psyche. It can be abused by the human ego, and it is more often than not misrepresented and misunderstood. For example, in *Volume One* of *Mary's Diary*, Blue is described as the most sacred Color Being and can transmit considerable healing power. It was summoned for use in the design of the Temple floor in Annica. Annicans receive the energy of Blue's holy gift by simply walking over the floor. It is offensive to Blue to be associated with the human adjectives "gloomy," "depressed," or "sad." Those words describe emotions and negative ones at that. The frequencies of Blue are all uplifting, and all of the hues excel in their activity. Blue has a known specific wavelength in the visible spectrum of light, one measurable way to observe its tranquil and soothing effect. All of Blue's flowers have qualities that cool or calm the mind and body—but only if you respect Blue and form a relationship with it.

The sky of Earth appears Blue because God wanted all the beings here to remember that peace and serenity abound. Gazing upon the sky strengthens humanity's connection to their Creator, Who had hoped that the words, thoughts, and actions of humans would be as pure as Blue's heavenly skies.

Humanity has poisoned itself by abusing Blue's manifestation as Earth's sky.

Truly, communion with a Color Being is ecstasy. Choose any particular color, the one you call your favorite, and start by addressing it with something like this:

> Oh, most blessed and radiant color
> of ______, you have been speaking to
> me for so long, and now I am ready

to understand more about you.

Show me how better to honor this life for the
sake of my connection to God, Who made
all. Show me your greatness, dear, ______.

Practice sitting still for five minutes, if possible, while
wearing the color you have chosen, and give complete
attention to your breath. If done with sincerity and rep-
etition, you will become aware of your breath taking on
the energy of the color that you called forth. Your body
will experience various shifts and tingles—some subtle
and some not so subtle—each time you commune with
the color.

After a time, your selected Color Being, as well as others,
will begin to show itself in marvelous ways. To know Color
as live and sentient Beings is one way to experience the
ecstasy of divine union on the physical plane. It is a deep
relationship, a form of communion, that lets you know
that the radiance surrounding you is a network of waves
of color and sound that is key to honoring and loving
humanity, Earth, and, most importantly, God.

Din's Commentary

There is no doubt about how Annie uses every minute
hue and shade comprising the vast array of the sentient
Beings of Color. For one thing, when she chooses to man-
ifest a form, it is one made of streams of the colors of
her choosing. Depending on her purpose and the work
at hand, she can change them all at will.

Holy moly! What was that?

Annie's Color Display

If I could translate color and vision into words like Stephen Hawking changes his thoughts into sound, I might be able to do justice to what just happened. However, I will not pretend that I am that good a writer, or maybe it's just that there are no adequate words in the human language. I will do my best.

The setting sun was luminous and full of Pink and Orange. It was the kind of summer sun that catches the eye and keeps your gaze no matter what you are doing. I have occasionally needed to pull my car over to the side of the road for safety because of the sun's brilliance at various times during the day, especially at sunrise and sunset. Today was a little different. Today, Annie took over the sun—just for a minute or so.

Daddy, you are so dramatic. I did not take over the Sun. I was simply having fun. What else am I supposed to do in this little solar system out here all by my lonesome?

All by your lonesome? Right, the big Kahuna of the universe, surrounded by an infinite number of Spirit Beings and an equal number of stars, planets, and galaxies, not to mention civilizations, is all by her lonesome. Poor baby. Please explain what you just did so that I don't have to, okay?

Well, to your eyes, I made the sun suddenly look like it was being swallowed by a swirling mass of spiraling rainbow light. Then I made the color mass appear to explode like the blast of a supernova, but a little more organized. The sun did physically change, but I did not allow the rest of the humans here to see it. I've done similar things with the sun before, and it created quite an uproar, so today, I did it for your eyes only. Isn't that the title of some silly song or movie? Never mind, don't answer that. As for my display, you know that all I have to do is blink my eye, and I can create or destroy whatever I want. I know how frustrated you get, stuck in your body here on Earth, with all its limitations, so I figured I would give you something fun to look at now and then. Not all that exciting if you ask me. Even so, none of your scientists will ever figure out how I made the Sun into an exploding vortex of color in one second, then brought it back to normal in the next — even if they could see it. That is because they have completely disconnected themselves from God, the One in charge of both creation and destruction throughout the Cosmos.

Watch this.

Five Seconds Later

Black took over the sky. Completely. For just a few seconds, there was no Sun, no Moon, no stars, no nothing. Everything was gone. But that wasn't Annie's doing. I could feel *Her* — Mother H — more than ever before. It was almost disturbing how strong her presence was just now, all over this planet. I know it was Mother H because the Black was *cleansing*. Yes, that is appropriate. While it is deep and dark, it is a cleansing sort of nothingness that gets rid of what does not belong while preparing the space for something new. My observation of Black was like a soul's experience at the moment before coming into a body. No, that's not quite right, either. All I can say is that Black as it just now appeared is what Mother H will do if humanity shows it is not choosing the path to its survival.

That was a shiver-causing realization.

Was that a taste of what's coming? If it was, then humans have no idea what's in store for them if they don't wake up and change their ways. I really hope that doesn't happen again. It was just for a few seconds, and then everything came back to the setting summer sun that I had been staring at before Annie had showed up.

Voila.

Why did you guys do that? That was just for me, right?

Grandma and I just wanted to give you something to describe. Yes, it was only for your eyes, but it was no joke. You just had a cosmic glimpse of the dimensional reality that humans will bring upon themselves because their behaviors and activities are obstructing the Creation Frequency. If you'd like, I can show you more. Your body now has the DNA required to receive visions of what's coming if humanity doesn't open its eyes. Consider this to be another wake-up call that you can share.

For now, though, I need to remind you that Grandma H is getting impatient. You are not doing much in your search for the Strong Weet, so I must pass the time by playing with the Colors to amuse myself. Why aren't you doing Intuition Development Circles or something so I can at least show up as an orb?

One more thing. I also need to remind you that Elise is Awakening rapidly and now has the ability to help locate the other Strong Weet. She is aware of her power and has been using it well, so just step out of the way for a little bit longer, okay? Give it a few days and then ask Elise to write about what she has been given concerning the Strong Weet. And get moving with the Development Circles, or I'll have to pull another Color event on you when you least expect it.

I never know what to expect from you anyway, Dear, so that's not very threatening. Nice try.

I think it would be a good idea to explain a little more about the Creation Frequency before you talk about the Strong Weet. I'm sure that many readers are still fuzzy on that subject, and they must all have an understanding of it.

Maybe we should let Elise handle that. It might be interesting to see what she comes up with. What do you think?

Good idea.

I want to talk about the development circles with her, so she'll be coming over this afternoon. I'll ask her to write the entry for the Diary then.

I have an appointment now, but I will check in later just to make sure things are moving along, Dear Father, and that you are not sleeping on the job.

All right. I'll see that Elise gets her assignment. I hope she can handle it. The Creation Frequency is key to everything, and we need to get that message across.

Elise still needs some experience, but I believe she will do well with this job. You might need to look in on her once in a while just to make sure she stays focused. Her conscious mind is a bit chaotic at times.

That should become a thing of the past as our DNA continues to activate within her. But Elise is different, isn't she?

Indeed. See you later, Father.

Bye, Annie.

ELISE WRITES OF MUSIC AND THE CREATION FREQUENCY

The passion I once had for Earthly music has died in me as I have awakened to the knowledge that much of this world's music is a blockade to the Creation Frequency and its vibrations are among the forces hastening the world's destruction.

Many readers will disagree. They will argue that music is awesome, that it is expressionistic and truthful, and that it can be masterful and peaceful. They will say that there is a whole range of what music can be, and people have the right to enjoy this different kind of language that humans have been creating since the dawn of time. They will point out that humans will never stop enjoying, performing, and listening to music. They will ask how music performed in places of worship can in any way be a disgrace to God.

The Creation Frequency consists of a multitude of energetic waves that flow together as a stream from deep space. The core of the Earth responds by amplifying and radiating the Creation Frequency throughout the heavens. This is how it has always been. This is the stuff by which all things in Nature can exist. Without the Creation Frequency, there would be no physical forms anywhere throughout the cosmos. All things that currently exist would disappear into nothingness if the Frequency were to be blocked or removed. The Creation Frequency is pure, eternal, cosmic God energy, generated and sent forth by Unconditional Love. All things living and non-living on

Earth, in this solar system, and the stars beyond are put together and function only because of the Creator God's Creation Frequency.

Does this Frequency have a sound? Yes. Music, for example is a malleable composition of living, vibrational energy. Unlike the Creation Frequency, it is not pure. It is not visible to the human eye even though sound, the wave upon which music rides, is a continuum of the energy spectrum that includes light. Instruments — organic and mechanical — generate these waves and give them form and substance when manipulated according to set notation. The energetic transformation is like water turning to ice.

Energy is never static but is always moving and is transmittable. Matter, in essence, is collected and condensed light. Matter is affected by all other forms of energy, especially sound frequencies. Music is destructive because it is deliberately manufactured and focused with no consideration for the Creation Frequency that sustains the universe. Every love song, advertising jingle, and mantra produced by humans pollutes the harmony of the Creation Frequency's cosmic stream. There are humans on Earth with spiritual origins from the darker worlds. They are fully aware of the effect of their music on the integrity and flow of the Creation Frequency. They also know that it is a tool to control the population by manipulating human minds.

Music cuts through reason and strikes directly at human emotions. Those who make music use that to their own purpose. Once released, musical vibrations travel throughout all of space and remain there forever, along with all the intended human and energetic effects whether good or evil.

At worst, human music is like throwing toxic acid at the

Earth and all its inhabitants. There are composers and producers who, consciously or not, use the vibrational currents of music to stupefy, dull, distract, and control humans into doing and believing what they want them to believe. Even music made without that intent causes distraction and allows humans to disconnect from God. That said, music exists that is in harmony with the Creation Frequency but it is rare in this world today. Choose carefully. Ask yourself these questions:

What is my favorite type of music?

Why do I like this music?

What fond associations do I have with this music?

If your answers are honest, you may surprise yourself.

***

Life on Earth exists within a low-energy physical dimension which gives the illusion of solidity. Humans have indulged in selfish and destructive behaviors for millennia with the result that they have lost the ability to access dimensions beyond their own. That loss has led people to believe that only those things that can be seen or heard in this physical dimension are real. Even so, humanity seems to have retained vague memories and impressions of what they were once able to experience directly. Many feel compelled to follow that trail, and their efforts range from scientific and pseudo-scientific studies to spiritualism and mediumship to witchcraft. Most people who engage in these activities are initially driven by simple curiosity. Unfortunately, it is far too easy to be seduced by ego and greed. What starts as an innocent diversion often descends to quackery and a quest for power over others. An interesting side effect of the increasing awareness of and interest in extra-dimensional matters is the proliferation of so-called authorities claiming to offer knowledge that bridges the gaps between spirituality and science.

The real danger buried in all of these activities is that some are adept at frequency manipulation and use it to keep the population ignorant of the true nature of the Creation Frequency and keep people separated from God. By propagating the lie that they can teach others how to gain and use individual personal power, they lead others into the trap of ego, causing harm to themselves and great damage to Earth.

I have told you all of this not to chasten or discourage you but to reassure you. Yes, you have become disconnected, but these words should encourage you to slow down and listen to what remains inside of you and in the created world around you. Those among you who are potential Support or Secondary Weet will know what I am talking about.

As for music, believe me when I tell you that True music awaits you not in this life but when you return Home. What passes for music on this world is just noise when compared to music not composed by Earth humans but is part of the very structure of Nature. When you hear it, you will not want to listen to any other kind.

***

Okay, my nose is itching furiously. That's what Annie does when she is trying to get my attention. My DNA is still in the process of Interfusion, so I am unable to see her the way Din can. It sometimes takes a while to realize that she is right here with me, which Annie and I both find frustrating. I am still learning to recognize her presence through physical touches and audible cues. I am just thankful that she is not slapping me on the back of my head the way she did to Din to get his attention in the beginning. Anyway, she's letting me know that I need to move on and tell the readers about the other two Strong Weet who have Awakened and will soon be joining the family.

ELISE TELLS OF MERTA

Merta is a humble individual who leads a quiet life not far from Annica. She has not yet Awakened to her true identity and abilities as a Strong Weet, but she soon will. This is the story of how Din and I discovered that Merta is one of the remaining seven Strong Weet.

After *The Strong Weet Society: Volume One of The Diary of Mary Bliss Parsons* became available, Din received a flood of emails from a host of intriguing individuals claiming to be "practicing witches." Many of them were angry and felt compelled to convey their disagreement with the book's declaration that there are fraudulent witches out in the world. They declared that the book had not taken them seriously and thus had insulted "witches" everywhere. Din was not surprised by this reaction as the book also predicted that many of these fraudulent witches would contact him to tell him that they knew themselves to be Strong Weet. The funny thing is that these angry individuals did not seem to realize that they were doing the exact thing that the book had prophesied. Din responded to some of the emails, but he consigned most of them to the non-existence of cyberspace by hitting the delete button.

It was not long, though, before the tide turned and the emails that flowed in were in complete support of Mary's Diary. Responses have continued to be positive since then, giving us great hope for our success.

One email caught Din's eye and went straight to his heart when he read it.

Hello. My name is Merta, and very strange things happened to me while I was reading your book, and even more now that I am done with it. I do not know what more to say than this, but this is good enough for now.

A deceased family member of mine, whom we have called *Pacha Mama*—not her real name—began to speak to me in Spanish as I was reading the messages of Mary in your text. While I was reading the English in the book, and hearing *Pacha Mama* in Spanish at the same time, I also heard laughter from someone who sounded like a young girl. I do not know what any of this is about right now. It is not disturbing to me, just very different. I don't know if you will even read this email, but I am glad to just write of it anyhow.

Regalos de Dios,

Merta Gonzales

When I told Din that *Regalos de Dios* means "gifts from God" in Spanish, we looked at each other and smiled. Merta had not asked for a response, and she had declared nothing for or about herself. She had simply shared a meaningful experience with a complete stranger who had written an interesting book. The simplicity of her message, coupled with the power of her experience, spoke strongly to Din and me.

"What if that was Maria speaking to her? Did she say what *Pacha Mama's* real name was?" I asked eagerly as I tried to read the email over his shoulder.

"No, she didn't. But it sounds as if God was translating the English words of the text into Spanish or His Holy Spirit was whispering other things to her as she read the book. Either way, I've got a good feeling about this one. I'll send her a quick response and hope she writes back. I'll keep a close eye on the emails."

Din became thoughtful, but after a few moments of silence, a smile spread across his face. I sensed it, too, and felt a smile forming on my own face. Then we both heard the unmistakable contagious laughter of Annie right there behind us as we re-read Merta's message. Annie laughed again and tickled us when we came to the part where Merta reported hearing the laughter of a young girl.

In *Volume One*, Din described how he, Mary, and Annie spent an Earthly life together as a human family — Jose, Maria, and their daughter, Anna — in Mexico. This email from Merta is a strong hint that she could well be a great-granddaughter of Jose and Maria's, perhaps even of Anna's, and who was now an adult living near us. If this were indeed the case, then Din and I also knew that we had found one of Din's long-lost granddaughters, who is, because of the direct connection, also a Strong Weet.

It took a few weeks, but we finally met Merta in person. When we did, she had some exciting stories to relate regarding her experiences leading up to her final discovery of *The Strong Weet Society*.

Merta's first adventure

Merta was taking her daily walk in the neighborhood park with her closest friend, Burro, the cockapoo. Merta and Burro enjoyed each other's company over anyone else's. Neither one of them liked to talk much, and Merta felt the dog was the most sensible of all Beings she had ever met anyway. They enjoyed the regularity of their walks and the simple repetitive trail they had been walking together for ten years. Rain or shine, sweltering heat or icy cold, Merta and Burro could be found strolling at Stephens Lake Park every day at one o'clock.

One day in late February, something incredibly different happened.

"*Dios! Que pase?*" Merta was suddenly aware that she was sitting at the edge of the lake with her naked feet in the water and Burro barking at her. There was no other person nearby. Merta, who never did anything out of the ordinary, had no memory of how she had gotten into the unlikely situation.

"What is this? Am I going crazy? Why am I sitting here like this?" Bewildered, Merta sat still and assessed her situation.

"I remember walking with Burro… *Si*, and singing the song that *Abuela* taught us:

> *Canta Madre*
> *de la Primavera*
>
> *Canta Madre*
> *De las flores*
>
> *Canta Madre*
> *De Christos*

And then, nothing. Now I find myself sitting here, *sino zapatos*, and Burro thinks that I am *muy loca. No se*, Burro, *no se.*"

She began to rise but lost her balance. She fell forward and landed on her hands, half in and half out of the water. Now she knew she did not feel right.

Suddenly, she was no longer lying in the mud at the

edge of the lake in the city park. Merta was standing in her *abuela's* kitchen, looking down at her muddy, wet feet and smelling the enticing aroma of fresh-baked *empanadas*. She heard a soft voice in the other room and recognized it as her *abuela* saying her daily Rosary.

"*Abuela?*" Merta, who was not frightened by the apparent time warp that had taken her forty years into the past, took a deep breath. Glancing down, she noted that she appeared as her adult self. That fact brought her some measure of relief.

"*Si, Merta. Donde estas?* If you are dirty again, *tu papi* is going to be very angry. You know that you are not supposed to be playing in *el lago* before dinner. I'm not even going to look at you, *mija*. Go wash up and come to say the Rosary. I am halfway done."

"*Abuela*, what am I supposed to do?" She had always looked to *Abuela* for guidance, so she instinctively called out to her for help in this strange circumstance.

Still hidden from view, her *abuela* said, "Know that you are returning to us, Merta. Be prepared to look for the ones who know you best. It is time to assist in The Great Plan, Merta. *Lee mi diario*. Read my journal. They are awaiting your return."

Like a movie screen going blank, her *abuela's* kitchen vanished, and Merta found herself again on the banks of Stephens Lake, feeling very strange indeed. Merta took another deep breath. She looked down at Burro waiting patiently beside her, and he looked back at her with his big chocolate eyes. "Burro," she said, and the little dog cocked his head to let her know he was listening. "There are very new things coming. I do not know what they are, but *Abuela Maria* has spoken, and we must listen very carefully to every sign. You will help me, *si*, Burro?"

"*Ruff!*" Burro replied, and the two of them began to

walk back to their home.

Along the way, Merta pondered the extraordinary experience and tried to make sense of it, "What do you mean *'mi diario?' Tu diario*? Your journal? I do not know of any of your writings, she muttered to herself. "*Ay, Dios*, what is this Great Plan, *Abuela*?"

Merta Contemplates Life and The Appearance of Pacha Mama

The supernatural event in the park had seemed familiar to Merta and yet impossible. Even though she decided that her experience must have been similar to the visions of some of the mystic Catholic saints, she did not go to her local parish priest to seek counsel. She decided that if Christ could be so patient and loving in the face of humanity's ignorance and evil, she could do her best to trust that this was a real message. She was a descendant of generations of those who knew how to be patient and maintain faith in the face of great mysteries.

Merta began to make a habit of going out with Burro at her side every dawn and dusk to watch the sunrise and sunset. She lived alone, as her only son was grown and lived a hundred miles away. Merta was accustomed to her solitary lifestyle and appreciated the silence of her blossoming crone years. Her most cherished activities were reading and spending time with Burro in her gardens. Even though she had distanced herself from much of the world, she explored it through books and so did not feel deprived.

She prayed the Rosary every morning using the wooden Rosary beads given to her by her *abuela* all those years ago. After that, she sent out her first thought of each day, "I ask of you, *Dios*, what would you have me do in this moment?" Then as the sun's first rays lit the dawn, she closed her eyes and felt herself swell like the tender shoots of the garden in the early warmth of spring.

Her answers came from nature. At first, they were just sensations of nurturing and growth. In time, she no longer needed to imagine herself as the little green things receiving sunlight, water, or the kiss of the breeze when she asked her questions of God. She found that communing with her garden brought her direct guidance from all the parts of the natural world—sun, earth, water, and air. She recalled how, when she was a child, *Abuela* had taught her the importance of knowing the connection of herself to all of Life:

"These Green trees have branches that work in the same way as all the parts of your body. Listen to the roots, mija, and as you grow, you will know that they have a purpose far beyond what anyone can see in this world. Never forget, mija, that you are not from this world."

Merta came to treasure her dawn and dusk conversations with her grandmother. She would take the messages from *Abuela* and ponder them throughout the day. Merta spent virtually every moment of every day in contemplation, although she did not think of it thus.

"I like to listen, Burro," she would tell her little dog. "Most people say they are thinking. I call it listening. I know that if I choose to listen, then I am not insulting *Dios* by talking in my head. That is why I have but one friend, and that is you."

Her joy in her life and her listening were enough to sustain her until dusk when a new conversation would commence with the setting of the Sun.

Abuela Maria comes to Merta's house

Those first few weeks of spring were a wonderful paradox for Merta, unique and yet expected all at the same time.

She ate in the way she knew the plants took their nourishment, steady but light. She became enamored with the idea that perhaps the time would come when she would produce her own food within her own body just by soaking in the sunshine and drinking plenty of water.

The visions of her grandmother increased, and Merta began to question which moments of her days were real and which were illusions. She had grown up immersed in the atmosphere of the Catholic faith. Her mother and grandmother had known the stories of many of the Saints and had recited them to Merta at bedtime since she was an infant.

"Knowing the stories of the holy ones who walked the Earth is as important as knowing when to plant different seeds. If you don't know this, you don't know how to feed yourself," her grandmother had told her repeatedly. *Abuela* was filled with such wisdom, and in her mind, Merta considered *Abuela* to be *Sant Abuela*. "Saint Grandmother" laughed whenever little Merta called her this.

✳✳✳

It wasn't long before *Abuela* was making regular appearances. She would sit on Merta's couch after observing the sunset, sip tea, and ask Merta if she had anything new to say.

Merta enjoyed these visits, but they puzzled her, too, "*Abuela*, what is this? Why are you here so much? I know I am not crazy, but does this have anything to do with me dropping into the lake. I felt like a donkey that day. Did you do that?"

"*Mija*, of course it was me. How else was I supposed to get your attention? Are you ready to talk?" Abuela looked as beautiful as she had forty years ago.

"*Si, Abuela.* Let me go get *mi horchata.* I just made some fresh, although the store did not have the rice I like, so I had to make the drink with a cheaper kind. I see you are already drinking. What herb do you have today?"

"No kind that you would know about, *mija.* Don't worry on that. I am here for more important talk." Abuela had never wasted time with trivialities. She was no different in spirit form. "Do you remember, at the lake, when you saw me back in our old home? You heard a voice that startled you."

"*Si,* there was something about someone looking for me and something about that Great Plan thing." Merta's thoughts were becoming less confused, and her body responded by relaxing and easing her aching back.

"That's it, Merta. The ones who brought you here are alive and well. You will go to them soon, and they will tell you of The Great Plan. You must read my Diary, mija, and pay attention whenever you are out in the world. You will know who they are when they appear." *Abuela* paused and smiled almost mischievously before she continued. "You have encountered these two once before in the most unlikely of places." *Abuela* vanished, leaving Merta with more questions than she had answered.

The ones who brought me here? Mami and Papi? No, Abuela said they are alive and well. What is this? Another one of Abuela's strange riddles, it seems. Well, at least these two, whoever they are, will tell me what this Great Plan stuff is all about.

Merta said the Rosary twice that day instead of once.

Merta is guided to Volume One

Abuela's visitations had Merta's feelings swinging between calm and agitation. She wanted to get her mind off the interactions for a while, so she gathered up her leather purse, patted Burro on his scruffy head, and said, "I will find a good book for us, Burro. This one will be special, and I will read it to you out loud when I get home. *Si?*"

She set off for the mall and the largest bookstore in town. Normally, she would walk right past the bookshelf displaying the new releases, as she was of the opinion that most current writers were mediocre, and she absolutely stayed away from all books about self-help or healing, which seemed to be the current fad.

Here.

Abuela again? Is that you telling me, 'Here?' Why now, *Abuela?* I just want some peace, and I want to find a good new book, so, por favor, just leave me be for a while, si? *Con respeto, Pacha Mama.*

Aqui.

Merta found herself staring at a book on the new release table. The image on the cover of the book was a painting of a mysterious, dark-haired woman.

Aqui.

The Diary of Mary Bliss-Parsons, Volume One, The Strong Weet Society.

Merta knew that she had found *Pacha Mama Maria*'s journal that she had been instructed to read.

Merta Remembers Seeing the Two

"*The Diary of Mary Bliss-Parsons: The Strong Weet Society,*" Merta slowly repeated the unusual title of the book that had just joined the ranks of her few prized possessions. She wondered about the word "Weet." What could it possibly be? She had never heard of such a thing. Somehow though, she knew it held a special meaning that had little to do with the usual trappings of this world.

"Grandmother, this is it. I know this is your *Diario.* I

do not know how you have written this, and I especially do not know who this DH Parsons person is or why he claims to have written your journal. I do know that you only speak truth, *Abuela,* and I know that this is it."

On the way home, Merta had to force herself to pay attention to her driving. She placed her purchase on the seat beside her. The image of the hauntingly beautiful woman on the cover of the book beside her drew her gaze, so she threw her jacket over it.

Merta arrived home and greeted Burro, who was asleep on her reading chair. "Burro, wake up. You will help me to solve this strange mystery about *Abuela's* messages. Let me get my tea, and I will begin reading to you." She continued talking to her friend while she went about the business of putting away her jacket and purse, making tea, and finally settling down in her favorite chair. "Somehow, from this book, I will understand what this is all about. But you know, Burro, this picture on the cover—it is strange. Something about it reminds me of *Pacha Mama.* That is why I was drawn to it, but it is not right. There is something just wrong about it. After I read this book, I will have something to say to this man DH. I will tell him that if he is going to be so bold as to write *Abuela's* diary—who is this man, *Abuela?*—then he needs to get her picture right."

Burro groaned, stretched, and hopped down to his blanket beside the chair. Merta sat down with a thud and opened the book.

Before she could read the first word, she started to feel tingly. "*Ay, Dios.* Hold on, Burro. I do not know where I am going."

She found herself in Walmart amid a disturbing and unusual event she had actually experienced two weeks earlier. She approached the fabric aisle to look for Blue flannel for a pillow she wanted to make and was startled to hear the sound of glass shattering in the entertainment section nearby. She looked up and saw not one or two but the entire row of televisions on the wall, all tuned to the same news report, blow up, one after the other.

People began running, and some shouted, "Call the police," or "It's a terrorist attack." Merta, however, did not feel panic. She felt disturbed, yes, but instead of contributing to the chaos, she squatted down, and rather than using her hands to cover her head, she folded them in prayer and began talking to *Pacha Mama*, asking her to pray to Jesus for peace on Earth.

It was noisy in the store, so no one could possibly have heard Merta's prayer. She did not want to break the flow of her connection to her grandmother in that moment, but she could not resist the urge to open her eyes and look around. When she did, she saw a man and a woman standing before her and looking straight at her. The woman was beautiful, and she was smiling as if nothing at all strange was going on. Her smile sent a powerful wave through Merta, causing her to lose her balance and fall over. By the time she righted herself and looked around again, the two were gone. "*Pacha Mama*, I have never seen Angels before," she thought. "Truly, I have been blessed this day."

Merta's head stopped tingling, and she found herself back in her reading chair. *The Diary of Mary Bliss Parsons: The Strong Weet Society* was on her lap and opened to page one, and Burro was looking up at her expectantly for her to begin reading. The cup of tea on the table beside her chair was still steaming.

What Din and Elise Saw That Day in Walmart

The day that Din and I first saw Merta, we did not know who she was. The entire experience was extraordinary, to say the least.

We were preparing for the first Intuition Development Circle and realized that the room's regular curtains were not sufficient to block all of the light from the outside completely, so we took a trip to the nearest Walmart to get some Black cloth to hang up over the curtains. We were immersed in the details of the Development Circle when the sounds of shattering glass and screaming people cut into our talk. I looked up at the row of televisions on the wall to my left and watched as they exploded one after the other down the line. People were shouting for the police and screaming about a terrorist attack.

"What the——" Din said and grabbed my arm and pulled me into the shelter of the fabric aisle. "This is no terrorist attack. Mother is raging right now," he said calmly. "Let's just wait it out and see what happens." He was smiling, and his eyes held a gleam of anticipation.

I took a cue from Din's behavior and inhaled deeply to calm myself. The noise and panic of the moment seemed to recede, and I heard a soft voice directly in front of me murmuring in Spanish. I looked down and saw a dark-haired woman with her eyes closed and her hands folded in prayer. In that same instant, she looked up at me. Her eyes grew large with wonder, and she lost her balance. As she collected herself, Din yanked me again, and we moved away.

I have learned not to question Din, especially in high-energy situations. As we got in the car and drove away, we both wondered what we would read about in the morning paper.

The Next Day

There was nothing in the morning paper about the exploding TVs in Walmart. I was surprised and curious about the lack of coverage. I called the local paper to inquire. I spoke with a reporter who had no idea what I was talking about. I hung up the phone and went to find Din.

"Why don't we call up Walmart to see what happened on their end," he said with a smile.

I finally got the manager on the line. I put the call on speakerphone and asked him what had happened with the exploding televisions yesterday. There was a long pause, followed by, "Lady, are you sure you've got the right store? I was on shift all day yesterday, and nothing like that ever happened. Can I transfer you to our regional office?"

"No, thank you," I said, hanging up the phone and looking at Din. Things were getting weird—or perhaps the correct word is "weirder."

ELISE MEETS SIT

In the course of my Awakening, I have acquired several very cool but sometimes disconcerting abilities, one of which allows me to see the personal energy fields of other people. Much of what I see is not pretty, and as a consequence, I have taken to avoiding most public places. I choose to stay at home and protect my sanity and physical well-being rather than risk exposure to the ugly and sometimes dangerous frequencies emitted by nearly everyone I encounter outside of the Annican land. Unfortunately, my duties often require me to leave the protection of that sanctuary.

On one of those days when my duties took me into the community, I finally crossed paths with Sit. The meeting was timely as I was in a state of emotional turmoil and discontent, but the essence of grace, love, and vibrancy radiating from her was instantly soothing. I soon learned that there is far more to this wondrous Being, and I thank God that she has appeared. I don't know what we would do without her as her presence on Earth, like that of Merta's, is critical to the success of the Great Plan.

The bookstore at one of the local colleges had recently begun stocking *The Strong Weet Society: The Diary of Mary Bliss Parsons,* and I had gone there to talk to the book manager about the sales. Part of my work with Din has been marketing and outreach for *Volume One,* and I regularly check in at the various places around town that are selling it.

The bookstore manager had been dismissive and said derisively, "Oh, that book? Yeah, I looked at it when it first came in here. I read the part about the end of humanity coming if I don't change my sinful ways. That author needs to get down off his high horse. I decided to help him out a bit by putting his book on the lowest shelf. You can see it over there."

His nasty attitude angered me and I huffed out of the store. Rather than taking a deep breath and getting my ego under control as I had been learning to do, I let my anger propel me toward the exit while I shot daggers from my eyes at all around me.

I was stopped at the door by the sight of a beautiful potted palm. I reached out and began stroking the long leaves. My anger evaporated as I remembered the story of Jesus riding into Jerusalem on a donkey and why Christians decorate their churches with palm leaves on the Sunday before Easter. This humble yet divine image soothed my temper and brought me peace. I breathed deeply and felt a shift in my head and heart. The love frequency coming from the plant was strong, but there was something or someone beyond that. I became aware of a wave of Blue-Green enveloping my heart, and I was not startled when I felt the soft touch on my left shoulder.

"Are you talking with the palm?" the woman asked. She had a delightful smile that reminded me of the way butterflies land on flowers.

"Um, yeah, I … I needed to stop for a moment to chill out, and it was calling to me." I usually would not have answered so honestly about the plant's communication but, somehow, I knew this person would understand.

Her eyes were sweet and brightly Hazel. They glittered with splashes of resplendent Blue mixed with ocean and rainy sky colors behind her eyeglasses. Her Silver-Grey hair shimmered in a way that was more of a glow than a sparkle. I blinked twice when my gaze met hers, but something let loose in my chest and head, and I instantly felt relaxed and wonderful. I laughed joyfully as the radiant, soothing wave from this unusual woman washed over me.

"Yeah, I have days like that, too," she said. "The plants help to get one back into one's proper place. In my line of work, I get to be with them all of the time. They truly are a wonderful family." Then she looked directly at me, extended her right hand, and said, "Hi, I'm Sit. What's your name?"

I am surprised that I had been so quick to answer her as her GLOW was beautiful and mesmerizing. From the moment I first sensed her presence, I seemed to be standing in two places at once. I was aware of standing next to a potted plant by the door of the Student Union listening to this woman named Sit. At the same time, I could see another scene projected over the first, but equally as real. In that scene, I was standing in an enormous cavern-like space next to a waterfall surrounded by unearthly flowers and towering plants. Somehow, I knew that the place was sacred. As the Sit standing next to me in the Student Union spoke, light streamed from her to the Sit sitting on a White rock and stroking a flower in the other world. The light streamed from one Sit to the other, much like the energy of Earth's magnetic field travels in loops between the North and South Poles. The other-world Sit looked a little different from the Earth-Sit—more Sit-like, perhaps—but their eyes in both worlds were identical Hazel perfection, swirling with indescribable color combinations. How did she get her eyes to smile like that?!

I knew, somehow, that this woman and I were connected.

"Uh, my name is Elise," I said, accepting her outstretched hand. As soon we touched, the double vision resolved, and we were once again standing firmly by the potted palm in the Student Union. "Did you say your name is Sit?" Then it dawned on me. "Oh, Sit. You must be the same Sit who is friends with Din Parsons. How wonderful to meet you." I couldn't shut myself up. "You spell that S-i-t, right? What a beautiful and unusual name."

"Yes, and yes. Din and I go way back. Most people think that my name is spelled S-e-e-t, or worse, S-e-a-t. How did you know?"

"I'm usually good with names — or spelling, I guess. I like languages. They are music to me, and I take care in listening."

There was an awkward moment of silence which we filled by petting the plant and smiling.

I spoke first. "Do you work here at the university?" Sit had an air of professionalism, and her ID tags were a dead giveaway, but I thought I'd ask even though Din had told me she was a scientist at the university.

"What kind of work do you do, and where did you say your name comes from?" I continued excitedly. She was beginning to feel like a best friend, and I did not sense that I was pushing any boundaries.

"Nature is my passion. I always wanted to be a forest ranger, but somehow, I wound up finding work in several different institutions assisting in labs doing medical research in various fields. It's almost as good as playing outdoors with trees. The lab I'm in now focuses on physiological functions at the cellular level. We're in the process of putting together a grant application to study molecular changes in cells in response to insulin. If we get the funding, it should keep us going until we all retire. I certainly hope so. I've always liked my work, and this job is the best one yet." She paused for a moment and looked at me, her forehead wrinkled with thought. "You talk really fast, you know. What was your last question?

Oh, yes, my name. Well, sometimes I tell people that Sit is short for Siddhartha Gautama—you know, the Buddha. Of course, I'd be lying if I told you that," she said with a hearty chuckle. "Actually, I don't know exactly where my name comes from. I grew up in southern California, and my parents were rather unusual people. Maybe it was the ocean and the desert air that got into their heads when I was born. Who knows? I just know that my name fits me, and I have always liked it."

Being with Sit was more than just easy or comfortable. It was like coming home. I had to find out more about her. Hoping for the opportunity to spend a little more time with her, I asked, "Is your lab on campus? Can I see where you work?" The bookstore was my last target for the day, and I had no further obligations. I also felt that by getting to know her better, I might get a few clues about myself. I felt a strange and wonderful friendship unfolding—but it certainly wasn't brand new.

"Sure, I have some time right now, actually."

We walked across campus to the Biological Science building. While I had taken some biology classes, I had never entered the part of the building reserved for research. Sit swiped her ID through a card reader on the door frame. "No one will mind you being here with me," she said. "Just don't go wandering off by yourself, or they'll ask you to leave."

I felt a rush of excitement as we entered the facility. I envisioned some sort of high-tech, futuristic laboratory like a scene from *Space: 1999* or something similar.

We walked down a long hallway lined with bulletin boards hung with colorful posters displaying the progress of studies on various aspects of cellular and molecular biology. I was intrigued by the graphs and pictures, but they may as well have been written in a foreign language, for all I could tell. We stopped in front of a door about halfway down the hallway. Using one of the keys in a bunch she had in her hand, Sit opened the door and invited me into a large open area subdivided into various alcoves and workspaces. I recognized some large equipment in one nook as a freezer and a refrigerator. A desk-height counter along one wall held several oddly shaped microscopes. The rest of the counters were of a height convenient for standing and held more equipment that I did not recognize. Various tools, glassware, and supplies were arranged neatly along the backs of the counters or on the shelves that lined the walls. The place looked more like a scene from *CSI* than *Star Trek*. I gradually became aware of a quiet hum thrumming throughout the lab.

Sit must have noticed me trying to locate the source of the sound because she looked at me curiously. "What's that sound?" I asked. "There's a strong vibration filling this room."

"You can hear that?" She didn't answer my question but said instead, "Come here, Elise. I want to show you something."

I followed her around a corner and into another set of alcoves that contained desks, computers, notebooks, and reference material. "This is where we figure out what we've been doing over in the other part of the lab," she said as she sat down and started waking up her computer.

She invited me to sit in the empty chair beside her, and I watched as she opened up files filled with numbers, pictures, graphs, and symbols whose meaning I could only guess at, let alone understand or describe.

"You asked to see what I do. Well, this is a small part of it." She turned to look at me and gave a short, melodic laugh. "Don't look so bewildered. As a musician and writer, you can surely appreciate these images as just another form of the language of the stars. The numbers in this file are raw data collected from our last set of experiments. These numbers are from various types of statistical analyses of the raw data. And finally, these graphs are attempts to make sense of the whole thing. I won't bore you with the details except to say that we have a way to go yet."

I caught my breath and didn't hear the last part of what she said. "How did you know that I am a musician and a writer?" I asked incredulously. *Did she really say, "language of the stars?" Mother, who is this woman?* I could hardly contain my excitement.

"Aren't you?" Sit said, looking at me knowingly. "Anyway, I see numbers and certain aspects of science as another way to…" she paused a moment, obviously wanting to choose her words well, "to stay connected and to talk about the wonders and variations in life. That's a simple way to explain my work. Isn't that what stories and poetry do—help people stay connected?"

"Yes, to both questions," I replied. "What I see on that screen is bewildering, and I am certainly unable to translate any of it. I agree, though. Math and science are languages with their own vibration—a link to the stars and beyond. The patterns of all those numbers and lines and words really are a foreign tongue, but while I appreciate this one, I don't think I have what it takes to learn it."

Sit smiled and said, "You and I have more in common than you think."

My eyes strayed from the computer monitor to the various items on and around the desk that uniquely identified the space as belonging to Sit. There was a small potted plant among the usual lab notebooks and reference books, a couple of apparently ordinary rocks, a few feathers, and four fairy figurines. What caught my eye, though, was the stack of papers next to the fairies. The cover sheet bore the title *Paranormal Investigations*.

I took the presence of the papers as an invitation and said, "So, your research goes well beyond human biology and normal science. I see that you are studying the invisible world as well. Din told me about all the paranormal work you guys have done."

"Studying? No. Listening and observing what comes to me, yes. I run a whole website on paranormal phenomena, and, really, sometimes I wonder if it would be better to direct my skills towards full-time work with the mysteries of things humans cannot begin to understand—well, that and gardening."

I touched the green-winged fairy statue and said, "Yeah, I know how you feel. I don't think many people know that plants are direct conduits to the stars and made from the same materials. I don't know much about astronomy, but I do know where plants take me."

The conversation was getting deeper and more revealing. Sit was focusing her gaze directly into my eyes, and I knew that I was in the presence of a powerful Being.

Then in the next moment, I felt Annie enter the scene, confirming that feeling. She swirled joyfully around the room, zipping in and out of the computer modules, dancing across tabletops, and sending rays of exuberant energy through my body.

Sit felt it, too. "Wow, she's back," she said. She sat very still for a moment, her face glowing with delight. "You're getting that, right?" she whispered without moving. Then we both broke out in laughter. Actually, it was more like giggles.

"You know her, too, huh?" I asked when I caught my breath.

"Yeah, she's been with me for a good long while, but I never know what she'll do next."

As if to prove Sit's point, the plastic skeleton hanging from the stand in the corner began to dance a jig.

"I've gotten used to friends visiting from the other side. There seems to be quite a few of them. I haven't felt any need to introduce myself to them formally, nor do I know exactly who they are when they communicate with me. It's just fun."

Annie streaked around the room one last time before she vanished. The only sign that she had been there was the right arm of the skeleton swinging back and forth.

The energy level in the room returned to something closer to normal, and Sit took the conversation in a different direction. "Say, Elise, I've been thinking about starting up another paranormal investigation group. The last one that Din and I organized kind of fizzled. There was nothing substantial going on, so we dropped the whole thing for a while. I have lots of good equipment to look into so-called hauntings, but it takes two or three to do it properly. I like what you said about listening, and I think you would enjoy it. I'm also hoping that you might be interested in participating in the Intuition Development Circle with me."

"What a coincidence, Sit. I was just about to ask you if you were planning to do any more paranormal investigations. By the way, I told you that I'm friends with Din, but I don't think I mentioned that I'm living in his mom's house on Annica. I've seen the magnificent gardens you created there. It is a wondrous space."

"It's an incredible place," Sit replied. "I can't take much credit for it, though. The Gardens are mostly the result of paying attention to the flow of energy and encouraging the plants to follow the pattern."

Sit looked thoughtful for a moment, then she said, "Din and I were speaking just the other day about putting feelers out for the others who would be joining us in a Development Circle. I feel like a sort of family reunion is about to happen, if that's not too weird to say."

"No, it's not," I agreed. "I feel that way myself."

It was time for Sit to get back to work, so we exchanged contact information and said our goodbyes. My meeting with Sit had exceeded all of my expectations, and I was elated. My thoughts raced as I walked back across the campus to my car. *She's one of us — perfect, masterful, and powerfully mysterious.* Only two questions lingered — has she read *Volume One*, and does she know who she is and where she's from? Surely, she must. She has known Din for a long time

The First Development Circle

Some weeks passed after Merta contacted me to let me know that she had finished *Volume One* and that while she was reading it, she had heard the laughter of a young girl and the voice of her deceased grandmother speaking to her in Spanish. Although Annie had played games with me by not telling me right away that Merta was a Strong Weet, I figured it out pretty quickly on my own. What she told me about the background and lineage of her Earth family and the humble way she described her encounters with her *Pacha Mama* were substantial clues as to her true origin.

Merta and I continued to correspond after that first email, but she was often slow to respond. I thought we could make better progress if we met in person, so I decided to invite her to participate in the Development Circle that I was planning to hold at my house in a few weeks. As I hit the send button to speed the electronic invitation on its way, I realized that there were now three more Strong Weet in my life. That made six counting Mary, Annie, and me. Only four left to find. Things have really progressed since this time last year.

Father?

Things are moving along. It seems like such a short time for nearly half of the Strong Weet to have made it into my life. What if —

Daddy, are you ignoring me?

Oh, Annie. Sorry. I was just so caught up in the flow of events and —

Please, just stop for a moment. I have to tell you some

things to help you prepare.

Okay, Precious, what is it?

When the Strong Weet show up for the Development Circle, the energy in your living room will be unusually intense — you will know what I mean when it happens. You are to watch Elise, Merta, and Sit very closely and pay attention to their responses from the first moment they enter the room. In some ways, their reactions to the heightened energy will have greater meaning than their assessment of the two paintings of Mother and me in your studio. Remember that while they may know that they are Strong Weet, they are not yet aware of the power and significance of that identitiy. When they encounter the energy in the room, they will know with certainty who they really are and will react with particular mannerisms and speech patterns. Once they pass the next test, the correct analysis of the paintings, you will be able to give them more information about the heritage of the Strong Weet. You must focus all of your attention on the first moments of this first encounter at the Development Circle.

Okay, I'm on it.

Later That Day

I was a little concerned about Merta as one of her recent emails seemed to express doubts about how I was involved with writing her grandmother's diaries. For this reason, I was doubly pleased when she used my phone number, which I had included in the emailed invitation to speak with me.

She spoke quietly and told me that she would attend the Development Circle, but only because "*Pacha Mama* told me I should go." I'm not sure if she really wants to come or if she feels somehow spiritually coerced into it. I'm happy she will be there with us, though, and I do not doubt that Merta will be quickly put at ease once she is immersed in the GLOWS of the other Weet.

I can understand Merta's reluctance at this stage. She'll be meeting with a group of total strangers in a total stranger's house. In this day and age, that can be kind of risky for a number of different reasons. Not to mention the fact that the things we will be getting into are, in the eyes of the world, more than just a little bit "out there." Even I am reluctant to invite strangers into my house before knowing much about them. If it weren't for the fact that Annie and Mother H have guided these women to us and will be close by while they are all here, I doubt that I would have agreed to start up this Development Circle business again.

This world has changed significantly since I last had a group like this in my house, and not for the better. You have to be careful who you befriend these days. You have to be careful how you talk to people. I may be going out on a limb to say this, but there is little goodness to be found in the majority of the people on Earth right now. They do not like what they hear from you if what you tell them disagrees with their not-goodness, and they may not even allow you to say it. My increasing involvement with The Great Plan has made it evident that this planet is on course to merge with the Book of Revelation. Because of the connection that Mary, Annie, and I have with God, it is easy for the three of us to understand the prophecies as they unfold daily. Even a regular human with no connection to God should be able to figure out what is happening in the world around them. I believe that anyone raised in a Christian family, attended church at least as a child, and has some knowledge of the Bible should be able to look around and know, or at least suspect, what's going on. That said, recent conversations with some of my Christian friends have led me to realize that many of them, just like the unbelievers, are ignorant when it comes to prophesy and the End Times. I hate to say it, but while there is much that I like about the Catholic Church, nearly every Catholic friend of mine is clueless regarding the Word of God and has no idea how all of the chaos and turmoil around them is going to turn out. It's even hard to have a normal conversation with them on those topics because they haven't read the Bible. My Protestant friends, however, know all about prophecy and are well aware of its unfolding these days. It seems that even the ones who haven't attended church and Sunday school all their lives are more open-minded and spend time reading the Bible and thinking about the scriptures on their own. I can usually have intelligent conversations with Protestants because they have a base to work from that ensures an in-depth discussion.

Catholics just get a whole lot wrong when it comes to what Jesus taught. They tend more to go with the emotions of the culture—especially on issues of social justice. Many Catholics tend to cave-in to the demands of whatever is popular in society while they abandon the Truths of what Jesus taught. I'm not talking about the list of *big* do's and don'ts found in the Catechism and learned by rote. I'm speaking of the subtler, little things that often prove to be more important than the so-called big things. Some Catholics, of course, are pretty well versed in scripture, and their devotion is to Jesus rather than to the Church. They are genuinely thoughtful and charitable Christians and refuse to join every liberal societal bandwagon that rolls by. Unfortunately, those truly devoted ones seem to be in the minority, and some of them are afraid to speak out for fear of being chastised by others in their Church. The bottom line is that all Christian denominations have their problems, but the Catholics should take a lesson from the

Protestants and open their Bibles for personal, in-depth study as the End Times come closer. If they don't, then I'm afraid they're going to be in for a big surprise in the not-too-distant future. Currently, there are two Catholics among the Strong Weet—Merta, and Elise. We will see how they react as things move forward. I think things will be easier for Elise than for Merta, though, simply because there is something about Elise that is different. She was raised a Catholic, but I don't believe the depth of her faith is limited to what she learned from her human teachers. I'm pretty sure it runs much deeper. There is something familiar about her that I can't quite put my finger on yet, but I'm going to figure it out pretty soon.

Friday Night Following the Development Circle

The addition of the black cloth to the curtains over the living room windows did an excellent job of blocking the light. There was just enough illumination from the two little table lamps for us to see each other and to avoid tripping over one of my poodles. I had a candle ready to use later during the Quiet Time, but I turned on the electric lamps because I did not want these Strong Weet to walk into a darkened room lit only by candles. I was especially concerned that Merta might turn around and never return if she saw such a sight. I wanted to make it clear that we were not about to engage in some pagan ritual. This was the first Intuition Development Circle, and it would set the stage for all future gatherings. The powerful energy frequencies that will be sent out could destroy the whole neighborhood if things weren't done carefully. Besides, I had no idea what Annie was going to do with the heightened energy she had warned me about.

Merta and Sit arrived at the same time and were properly announced by the barking of the poodles. Elise had arrived a few minutes earlier and was busy wrapping some objects in cloth and putting them in paper bags for the psychometry exercise we would be doing later. I was excited about the evening's potential. The whole thing could be a big bust or a real eye-opening experience.

The poodles calmed down as soon as I opened the door to Merta and Sit. I wondered at the synchronicity of their arrival. Merta, the shorter of the two, is a middle-aged Mexican lady with brown skin, black hair, and a slightly rounded figure. She wore a modest, deep green dress that fell to her ankles. I also noticed that she wore a gold cross and a silver Virgin Mary medal on a gold chain around her neck.

Sit, lean and tan from hours spent tending the Annican Gardens, was also shorter than average. She was dressed professionally in slacks and a button-up blouse. She held a strange-looking amulet in one of her hands.

I returned their smiles, greeted them, and welcomed them into my home. I had prepared to be formal — to get everyone introduced and seated quickly and start off by explaining what we would be doing that evening — sharing our personal paranormal experiences, the psychometry exercise, and the Quiet Time. Upon meeting Merta, however, I realized just how strange these activities would seem to her. I decided I'd better just relax, take it slow, and let everyone get to know each other a little first. I could tell that Merta was uncomfortable. In her emails, she had continued her polite probing to find out more about me personally and if I knew anything about her grandmother, Maria Gonzales. She seemed upset and confused about me but was not shy about telling me that this grandmother of hers, *Pacha Mama*, was directing her to communicate with me. She did not understand why I had written the diary of her grandmother. I could see how weird this might be for her. I knew it was a huge step for Merta to even show up at my house.

Elise, who is half Filipina, and Merta, who is all Mexican, began to speak in Spanish, so I turned to Sit. I don't understand why it is that Filipinos speak Spanish, but then Elise's father had also had an Italian first name, Pacelli. Go figure. More often than not, this little world called Earth doesn't make a lot of sense.

Anyway, I was happy to see that Elise seemed to be putting Merta at ease, and I turned to Sit. "That's a very unusual amulet." I was curious about it and wondered why she brought it.

"It belonged to my great-grandmother and is part of a unique family tradition. Only the women in my family have ever touched it. It was given to me by my mother three days before she left her body."

"I suppose I shouldn't touch it then. Of course, now that you are the keeper of it, you could make an exception for me," I said playfully, knowing that she would not.

"Not on your life. That would tarnish the energy forever," she said. "And besides, I don't know if you could handle the power it conveys."

The oval amulet was about the size of the palm of Sit's hand. It appeared to be made of silver and set with small Blue stones. Sapphires? I couldn't quite make out the odd design etched into the surface as she kept her fingers curled over it.

"I brought it to this gathering because I thought there might be an energy here similar to what I have experienced while using it on my own. It's more of a personal tool, but I was curious to see what might happen in this setting."

Hmm, a personal tool inherited from the women in her family. Another indication that even though she is still unclear about her true identity, she does have some awareness. I have known Sit in this life longer than any of the other Weet, but I have only recently begun to notice the evidence of her Strong Weet essence. But then, I didn't even know who I really am until about a year ago.

"Can you at least hold it up so I can see its detail?" I wanted to see this object that had been used for generations with a conscious level of knowing and power.

"Okay, but you have to promise not to touch it."

"I wouldn't dream of it," I said and made a show of putting my hands behind my back to prove my point.

She opened her right hand and raised the amulet to where I could get a good look at it. The surface of the silver medallion was decorated with an intricate pattern of lines, loops, and whorls. Seven brilliant Blue sapphires of varying size were set into it at points where some of the lines intersected. The pattern picked out by the sparkling Blue stones seemed vaguely familiar.

"Is there a significance to the pattern made by the sapphires?"

"That's not entirely clear. All I know is what I heard from my mother and grandmother. Grandmother said that it's a map to the star we came from. I'm not sure what that means, but I do know that the Earth has never really felt like my true home."

Elise and Merta had stopped talking to each other and turned their attention to the amulet in Sit's hand.

"That is exquisite," Elise exclaimed, her eyes wide with wonder. "I bet that came from the women in your family."

"Blue sapphire was my grandmother's favorite gemstone," Merta said, equally enthralled. "She had so many that my grandfather used to tell her she was stealing from the ocean at night just to get the stones."

The pleasant, ice-breaking conversation had relaxed everyone but had not prepared us for what came next.

Ten Minutes Later

Now, Father.

With Annie's words, the room turned liquid. The walls, floor, furniture — everything — melted into blindingly beautiful flowing streams of Gold. A vibrating, pulsing sound like a giant heartbeat filled the room with what I recognized as pure Creation Frequency streaming from God. So, this was the heightened energy that Annie had promised.

I have become used to this sort of flash, instantaneous experience. I wasn't sure about my three new friends, though, and it certainly wasn't the moment to ask them.

I glanced up at Elise. She still appeared human, but her form was beginning to vibrate and ripple with Purple, Green-Blue, and crystalline swirls of Gold. Sit was exploding in cascades of Pink, Green, and Yellow lights. Sitting next to Sit, Merta was engulfed in waves of oceanic Turquoise while Magenta pulsed around her heart. It was a superbly beautiful moment, mostly because I knew that we shared a vision given to us by Annie straight from her mind.

An experience like this would have sent many people fleeing in terror. Instead, when it ended about five seconds later, all three women wore the kind of expression seen on the face of someone who has just ridden a roller coaster for the first time — joy, exhilaration, bewilderment, relief at having survived, and something that says, "Can we do it again?"

Even though I knew this had been a shared vision, I wondered what each woman had experienced and how each had been affected.

Watch and listen, Annie whispered.

"Well, I guess I won't be needing this amulet after that," Sit said and tucked it carefully into her pocket. Then she smiled with warmth and affection as she looked at each of us with newly recovered recognition. "How good it is to be with you all again. Why has it taken so long for us to get together?"

Sit's Awakening had begun.

"*Dios mio. Pacha Mama* does not need to convince me anymore about any of this. I think we might need to bring another chair out here with us for her." Then Merta started mumbling something under her breath. Elise leaned forward to listen, and I observed while Merta used the middle finger of her right hand to trace what looked like the numeral five inside a circle on her chest.

I couldn't believe it! Where did she learn that? Does she know that the image she just drew is a sacred symbol of our Homeland, Hectarus, and a dedication to God? The number five inside a circle — of course, back Home, it isn't a numeral but a sacred symbol meaning something entirely different. One magical revelation after another and this is only the beginning. A joyful sense of strength and camaraderie took root and grew as we each shared our impressions of the experience.

We soon settled down, and I was able to launch into my planned description of the Development Circle and how it would assist us as individuals and as a group. I explained that we would do the psychometry exercise first, then finish up the evening with the Quiet Time, during which we would welcome our loved ones to join us if they could. Merta was already communicating with her grandmother frequently, but I didn't know how much intuitive frequency these women were capable of. Catholics do this sort of thing all the time when they talk to the Virgin Mary or any of the hundreds of recognized Saints. Really, no Christian, Catholic, or Protestant should feel uncomfortable at any of our meetings. The exercises we do are more like having simple conversations with our loved ones who now reside in Heaven and have nothing to do with psychic mediums or conjuring ghosts. I've heard many Christians say that they speak with their dead sister or brother or father or spouse all the time when no one is around to hear them do it. These exercises are no different, and they will be a regular activity at our DCs. My hope is that they will contribute to the Strong Weet's natural abilities.

Before we got into these activities, though, I told Merta and Sit of Mary and Annie's portraits in my studio. Now was the time to test their perception of the images. There was no need to test Elise as she had done that previously, confirming her status as a Strong Weet.

Then I began to wonder.

Annie, do we even need to do that part now, after what just happened?

Do it.

When Annie says *Do it*, there is no choice but to obey. I guided my new Weet buddies outside to my art studio, where the two paintings of Annie and Mary hung on a wall ready to be evaluated, and opened the door. Merta and Sit looked at them in silence for a moment, then simultaneously broke out in laughter.

"If that is supposed to be *mi Abuela*, you better get ready for a big flan pudding to come flying onto your face, Mister Din. Do not tell me that you painted that to be her?"

"Yeah, I don't know who that woman is in your painting, but I do know that it is on the cover of your book," Sit said, rubbing her index finger over her lip before she spoke again. "I hate to criticize your artistic abilities, but that is not the image of Mary that I had in my mind. That one of Annie looks way off, too. Were you self-medicating when you painted them or is this intentional?"

Wait a minute. First of all, I couldn't remember if I even had said they were to identify the flaws in the paintings, but here they were, coming out with astute and correct observations that only the Strong Weet could have. They didn't identify defects. They simply stated that they did not believe the portraits to be those of Mary and Annie.

I said nothing but waited, just like Annie had told me to do, and watched Sit and Merta walk around the studio. Elise had wandered off into the yard and appeared to be talking to the Linden tree, and then she disappeared. Things were definitely beginning to change.

"I'm not into self-medication. And I think those paintings are pretty darned good. I worked hard on those things," I said, playing the role of the offended artist.

"Baloney," Merta muttered under her breath.

"Baloney?" I protested.

"We're sorry if we offend you, Din," Sit said. "I mean, they do resemble Mary and Annie to some degree, but there are all kinds of problems with those portraits."

"Yada yada," I muttered, keeping up the act but secretly pleased that both Weet had passed the test with no coaxing or guidance.

It was hot and crowded inside the little studio, so I suggested that we all go back inside and have a glass of iced tea. Just as we reach the back door, Elise showed up carrying a gallon jar full of tea. *Can she read minds now, too?* I thought.

Elise's cloudy brown tea looked like sludge water, but she was smiling as she said, "I made a special infusion for our gathering if you'd like to try some. It's made with nettles, oat straw, red raspberry leaves, burdock root, rhubarb, and dandelion root, and it's been steeping for about two hours now. Don't worry. It tastes better than it looks."

"She's gonna kill us, Annie," I thought as I looked

around, hoping that my precious Daughter would come to our rescue. I've had Elise's tea before, and—

Hush. As usual, Annie's voice came out of nowhere, but her words were meant only for me. *You could learn a thing or two from Elise. She knows quite a bit about healing. You may need her help from time to time, you know.*

"Oh, that is a combination I have never tried." Merta seemed interested. "Is it good over ice?"

"I'll have a glass, too," Sit said. "It does look a little ominous, so make it heavy on the ice."

I considered the state of my bladder and gastrointestinal tract and refused the offer of tea. The women stopped briefly in the kitchen to gather glasses and ice and pour tea. We finally all made it back to the living room, and I announced that it was time to settle in again to the flow of the Development Circle.

We took our places according to the plan Annie and I had worked out. The room contained a sofa and a love seat arranged against the two adjoining outside walls. These could be viewed as forming one half of a circle. In addition, four folding chairs were set up in the open area of the room, completing the circle. The arrangement provided seating for all of the Strong Weet present this evening and the undiscovered Strong Weet who will be attending in the future. Annie had directed me to arrange the seating as if everyone were present so that the Strong Weet energy would begin to accumulate even in the absence of the others.

"Why are there so many chairs here?" Sit asked.

"Well, we do need an extra for *Pacha Mama,*" Merta said. "One of them is for her, right?"

"Yes, Merta," I said. "The spot where you sit tonight is where you will always sit for these gatherings, and where each of you sits relative to the others is important, as well.

Merta, your seat will be the first folding chair next to the love seat, and *Pacha Mama* will sit in the chair next to you. Sit, your place is at the left end of the long sofa. Elise, you are in the middle, next to Sit, and I will sit at this end next to Elise. When the other Strong Weet join us, they will have their assigned places as well. Remember your spot and never sit in anyone else's. That will maintain the purity of the energy that will accumulate with each DC and amplify it a hundred-fold. Now, let's get this show on the road."

"So, we're like a big, circular generator right here in the living room," Sit said.

"Right," I said. "And you'll learn about that and more as we go forward with your development—which is precisely what a Development Circle is all about."

It seemed that the carefully planned seating had the effect of uniting and focusing everyone's attention. The room was quiet now, and the Strong Weet seemed as ready to proceed with the exercises as I was to lead them.

"Now that I have your complete attention, our first order of business will be the psychometry exercise. Here's how it works. We're going to pass around a brown paper bag containing an unknown object. You will not be looking at the object, and I don't want you to try to peak in at it. Don't squeeze the bag to try to feel what the object is. Don't try to smell it or shake it or anything else like that. What you should do is register in your mind the first impressions you get when the bag is in your hand. That's all. It may be a color, an image of a person associated with the object, a place, or just about anything. The important thing is to remember that first impression. Keep silent until everyone has had a chance to hold the bag. Don't reveal your impressions until it is your turn to do so. There's no time limit for how long you hold the bag, but we don't want to be sitting here all night, waiting for one person to finish. Okay? Then we'll round-robin and give everyone a chance to share their intuitive impressions. Don't ask the person speaking any questions. Just allow them to have their turn, and we'll save interactions for after. Got it?"

Elise put the first brown bag on the coffee table in front of us, setting it down carefully so that there would be no sound of the object moving inside the bag or striking the table. She would not be participating in this particular exercise as she was the one who had selected the item. I had instructed her to watch Sit and Merta as they held the first bag and mentally note anything of relevance and share it with me later. I had no idea what objects Elise had chosen, so I included myself in the exercise just to contribute to the collective experience.

Everything went according to plan, and Merta and Sit proved beyond a shadow of a doubt that they were well on their way towards knowing their true nature. As fun and enlightening as this exercise was, the Quiet Time proved to be the highlight of the evening. I am still awed by Annie's powers, even though I have seen a lot of what she can do.

"Um, before we do the Quiet Time, I really need to use the bathroom," Elise said as she stood up.

"Do you by chance have two bathrooms? That combination of herbs in Elise's tea seems to be quite the diuretic. I really have to go, too," Sit said.

"Please hurry," Merta chimed in. "I don't think that combination is too good for my bladder, either."

I shook my head and said to the others, "We could probably use a break about now, anyway." In my head, I said to Annie, "Boy, am I glad I got out of drinking that stuff. Elise is gonna kill me one of these days with all of her plant medicine. Are you sure she's safe to have here?"

It would do you good to drink what she makes. These ladies are smarter than you.

Very funny, dear Daughter. Very funny.

Can't you take a little joke?

Humph.

While the ladies took their turns in the bathroom, I got up to stretch my legs, then we all settled back into our places for the Quiet Time.

Elise lit the single candle sitting on the coffee table in the middle of our "circle." I reminded everyone that we would be calling forth any loved ones interested in joining us for the evening. This exercise was really for the benefit of the new Strong Weet and should augment their natural attunement to things humans classify as paranormal. I anticipated another event similar to what we had all experienced at the beginning of the DC, although there is never a way to predict what Annie will do.

I was to stay alert, once again, to the women's responses and take note of everything that occurred. I realized this exercise might seem like a joke to Merta, who was used to communicating with *Pacha Mama*, but this was not about contacting spirits. The purpose of this exercise was to give the Strong Weet a taste of what their lives will be like from this moment forward.

Even now, as I write these words and reflect on the events of that evening, I have to say, again, that I am amazed at the power of my sweet daughter, Annie. One would think that I would be used to it by now, but the girl keeps doing things that are utterly impossible in this earthly realm. If seen by the average human being, her normal activities would cause that person to pass out immediately — or worse. Annie is pure light and energy. She is the highest vibrational Being anywhere throughout all of the universes, and ordinary people would not be able to withstand her presence.

I scanned the circle of Strong Weet to gauge their readiness. I nodded at Elise, and she spoke our intentions to God, letting Him know that we gathered in reverence to communicate with or receive from any loved one who wanted to join us for the evening. This was more of a formality, as God is all-knowing, but it is done out of respect and to remind us of the seriousness of our undertaking.

Elise finished, and the room fell silent. No sound leaked in from the outside, and even the poodles were still. Then things began to happen.

The flame of the candle on the coffee table started to weave back and forth, even though I had been careful to eliminate any source of draft in the house when I prepared for the evening. We all noticed the movement but kept quiet. Slowly, but definitely, the yellow-orange flame swayed left to right in a mesmerizing rhythmic pattern. A feeling of deep peace and comfort filled the room, and we all settled more comfortably into our seats.

I knew that the Weet brimmed with excitement at this activity so early in our Quiet Time. I was impressed that they were able to remain silent and maintain their calm.

As we continued to watch, an orb of pure White light appeared over the flame, which had ceased moving and elongated to connect to the orb. The small Blue-Purple center around the candle wick streamed up through the vertical flame and into the White orb as well, so that what we saw was a narrow flame with a Blue-Purple core shooting up and into a glowing ball of White light.

The sound of Elise's haunting, resonant Hum penetrated the silence, and the orb responded by increasing in size. The energy of the Hum appeared to be feeding the orb. The ball of light expanded quickly from the size of a softball to that of a basketball. As the Hum continued, the orb expanded quickly to two feet, three feet, four feet, five feet until it reached the perimeter of our circle and exploded. We all shielded our eyes but were able to see the brilliant White ball shatter into a myriad of tiny, prismatic filaments of light. The spider-web thin lines of cosmic light shot out from the orb like thousands of pristine crystalline fibers of pure light energy launching out in every direction, filling the room and going beyond the walls and ceiling. Then the cloud of light collapsed and coalesced into a recognizable form. It was Annie! She presented herself to the little group of Weet as a three-dimensional form made entirely from transparent, glowing crystal. She stood before us in the middle of the room, feet on the floor and head touching the ceiling. Running streams of Purple, Blue, and shimmering Gold were visible as throbbing veins and arteries within her White translucent body. Her hair was a flowing combination of Amber and Gold with streaks the color of cherry wood. Her eyes—my heavens, Annie's eyes have the same energy that her mother, Mary, has in hers. At this moment, they are Blue, but I have seen both Mary's and Annie's eyes change color at will, so it is impossible to say that they are any one color. They are whatever color they want them to be.

Annie shimmered and shrank to more normal size and hovered over the candle flame, which had also returned to normal. She had modified her appearance to make it easier for the Strong Weet in the room to get to know her and was wearing a modest, light Blue dress that covered her from throat to mid-calf.

She looked at me, and I heard her whisper into my head, *Get on with it, please.*

I looked around the circle and saw that Merta was wearing an almost comical expression of astonishment—open mouth, bulging eyes, and all. She clutched the cross that hung around her neck in one hand and held her other hand tight to her chest. I sent her a quiet, "It's okay, Merta," to reassure her, as I had no idea how she would handle this.

I could not see Sit directly as Elise was sitting between us. Elise told me later that she heard Sit's breathing get deep and full as we watched Annie emerge from the orb. She could also tell that Sit's eyes grew wide as well and that she was smiling with a grin that practically consumed her face, as Elise put it. She also said that Sit seemed to be enjoying herself.

Annie gave us just enough time to react before she spoke again.

I have to go to the bathroom. I drank some of that tea Elise made while I was waiting for all you guys to get ready, and you're right. That stuff is potent.

We all broke down and laughed. A Spirit Being needing to pee—she was joking, of course. Then Annie pulled a "Mother H" on us and grew suddenly. She shot up through the roof of the house until her head was about thirty feet above us, and we were left staring at her glowing feet.

Merta gave me a concerned look but maintained her calm. "Can your neighbors see this?" she asked, then we all laughed even harder.

"No, this is just for us," I assured her. I was happy to see that Merta was more relaxed and had let go of her chest. She was, however, still holding on to her cross.

"We are so happy that you have joined the circle tonight, Annie dear," Elise said when we had regained our composer. Is there anything that you want to tell us?

Annie replied in the sweet voice of a child, and not that of the most dangerous and powerful Being ever created:

Yes. I want all of you to know that the Mother of

Humankind, myself, and your Creator God are delighted that you have finally come together. There is much work to be done, and more patience is necessary as we are still waiting for the other Strong Weet to join us. Dear ladies, as you are now fully aware of who you are, I will be visiting with you individually soon. I have specific messages for each of you, and I will appear in a way that will not alarm you and that you will recognize as me. I will see you all again as a group when you come together for another DC. In the meantime, be sure to stay in touch with each other. The circle is strong now and will grow stronger.

"Is that all?" Elise asked.

Most importantly, keep your noses clean.

Annie's form became a swirling vortex of Gold and Silver and went up and out through the roof like a tornado in reverse. As the last tail of light disappeared, a shower of Yellow sunflowers fell through the ceiling. They seemed to be quite solid, but when Sit reached out to catch one from the air as it fell, her hand passed right through it, and the flower disappeared.

Thank heaven she didn't leave that mess in my living room. It would be just like her to make those flowers real, so I would have to clean them all up.

Later that night, I turned on the bedroom light and found my bed covered with fully blossomed sunflowers.

Three Days Later

Where is Mary? She seems to have disappeared from the universe, or at least from the arena of my perception. I've called out to her but have gotten no answer. I'm beginning to think she's mad at me for something, or maybe that I've done something so stupid she doesn't want to be around me anymore.

Nonsense, my dear.

Mary? Where have you been? Why have you been gone so long? I can't say, "I've missed you," because I know that you are always inside me and all that, but I haven't heard you in such a long time.

I have been both within you and watching you from afar at all times, Din, and you have been doing precisely as Mother H has guided you to do. We are all quite pleased. I have refrained from speaking with you for a while so that you could focus on the tasks at hand and gather in the new Strong Weet. Don't worry. We are inseparable. Or have you forgotten?

Of course, I haven't forgotten. It's just so good to hear you again. So, what's up?

I just wanted to let you know that there is purpose behind my staying away for more extended periods now. Do not be alarmed by my apparent absence, for I am becoming ever closer to you and all of the Strong Weet even though you will not see or hear from me for a good long while. You will understand this in time.

I'm not sure I like the sound of that, but I suppose I must accept it. I know that Mother H and THE GOD OF ALL have everything mapped out perfectly, so I will just have to trust that your being away is good.

Just remember, everything is going perfectly, but we must continue to stay alert and pay attention to every detail, Din. That is enough for now. I must go. There is much to do.

Just be sure you give me a nod once in a while to let me know that I'm doing this right.

I will. And never forget, Annie is here with all of you at all times unless she is called away for an emergency. There is an entire universe out there, you know.

Indeed, I do, Mary. I also know that this tiny little planet called Earth is a big part of that universe right now. I just hope our Weet can pull through for us.

Not only the Weet, dear. Humanity must be represented in the decisions as well. Remember the directive. Unless a certain number of humans are supportive, God no longer cares to sustain life here, and why should He?

I hope it doesn't come to that.

It will not if we all do our tasks well. I must go now, but I will not be far from you.

TRUE POWER IS EXPLAINED

Elise offered to cook a meal for us to share before getting down to business on the evening of the second gathering of the Strong Weet. I agreed that it was a good idea as there is no better way for people to get to know each other than over good food lovingly prepared. My plan was to give Merta and Sit further instruction regarding their true nature and the power that flows through them because of it. Sharing a meal would go a long way toward developing the camaraderie that will be key to the Strong Weet's understanding of their origins and the part they will play in the execution of The Great Plan.

The night of the dinner meeting was stormy with heavy rain and wind. I considered calling it off as I was concerned about the safety of driving in such conditions. However, Mother H never does anything without a good reason — even sending storms — so I didn't worry about it too much. Also, neither Merta nor Sit had contacted me to express any concerns. I did get an email from Elise to let me know that the meal preparations were well underway. When it comes to their work, the Strong Weet are like the Post Office, "Neither snow nor rain nor heat nor gloom of night ..." Nothing would stand in our way or alter our plans. In fact, we could stop a hurricane if necessary.

Merta and Sit arrived on time and safely. I was not surprised when they each reported that the downpour stopped as soon as they got in their cars and that neither had any trouble getting here to Annica.

Everyone quickly settled into their assigned places around the living room. I took a deep breath and felt a surge of peace and comfort from the presence of these three women. This was indeed the beginning of the family reunion I had long been awaiting. My job now was to find the precise words that would charge each one's memories so that they would all feel this connection as I do. Merta and Sit had revealed much of their attunement and character at our first Development Circle, so I felt sure that I would see similar expressions regarding their awareness of our connectivity.

There were some additional Spirit Beings with us that night, and their presence gave me the confidence of knowing that what I had to say would come out exactly as it should. All I had to do was take a deep breath and begin speaking.

A few Spirit Beings of a truly holy nature sat in on our meeting. They smiled lovingly at all of us from their plane of view as they observed the circle. A glance at Merta and Sit told me that they were aware of the other Spirit Beings in the room, but they could not see them the way I could. Elise sat on the couch next to me, crocheting quietly. She was smiling, and I knew that she was conversing with our spirit guests in her own subtle way. Thus far, Elise was the only Strong Weet who I was sure could see spirit beings the way I can. I was hoping it wouldn't be long before the others could do so as well. And by "Spirit Beings," I do not mean "ghosts."

99% of the time, so-called ghosts are figments of the imaginations of those who claim to have seen them. The residual energy that appears as a semi-transparent, cloudy form now and then is not a living thing. It's just an echo—a remaining spark released by a bit of life before the permanent change occurred. When a person dies, his body is left behind to disintegrate into various elemental components. One of two fates awaits the spirit of that person. It may be transported to the person's home of origin or be annihilated and released into the vast recesses of dark space. Yes, a person's spirit can return for a visit now and then if there is a need or purpose. However, they do not return to Earth willy-nilly every time someone demands they do so, nor do they appear in physical form or ghostly imagery. They return as energy beings and are invisible unless their appearance is somehow necessary to The Great Plan. They communicate with their loved ones by making a mental connection. Some humans are sensitive to the presence of the spirit beings, but the only Beings on this world that can actually see human spirit beings are the three Created Beings.

The meeting begins

"We are here this evening primarily to honor God, as is the case whenever we meet like this. I have much to share with you this evening, so this meeting will be more of a lesson than a discussion. My goal tonight is to remind you of your true heritage and not your earthly one. I'm sure that what I have to say will raise questions, but I ask that you hold them until I finish. It is best to get through this without interruption, as many of your questions will be answered as I speak. There will be plenty of time to ask questions and share your thoughts at the end of the lesson.

"Elise and I have done a lot of work to ensure your presence here with us at this moment. Be assured that other Strong Weet and some of the Secondary and Support Weet will be attending these meetings in the future. They will be joining us as they Awaken, and the strength and nature of their abilities and their loyalty to The Great Plan are determined. Loyalty is especially important to God and primarily requires that The Great Plan be regarded seriously and that you remain silent about who you are and what you are doing. This is not an Earth-based church or any sort of bizarre cult. The knowledge we possess is to remain ours alone until it is time to put it to use. Remember, this has nothing to do with ego or self-gratification. It is all to divert a world disaster that is, for now, scheduled to annihilate Earth and everything and everyone on it. We must remain focused.

"Looking around the circle, I see expressions of wonder and possibly even fear. Please, *do* be filled with wonder, but do *not* be afraid. You will all learn this evening that there is nothing for a Strong Weet to fear. What I am about to share with you is of great importance. You have never heard anything like it before, but I assure you, it is pure Truth.

"To begin with, Hectarus is the name of your home world. Humans call the star system in which Hectarus lies, the Pleiades, but those who originate from there call the entire star system, Hectarus. The word "Pleiades" is not used back home. Of greater importance, Hectarus is a part of what humanity has called "heaven" for the past two hundred millennia. It is not, however, the Heaven to which all beings return when they leave their bodies. The humans of the planet Earth originated from many different star systems, and each human will return to their original star system when they pass from this life. Their home planet is, in effect, their Heaven. Each being's return to their Heaven is dependent on the life they led on Earth and the degree to which they acknowledge God and abide by His Will.

"You Strong Weet are direct descendants of the original Hectaran Founders who assisted in the SEEDING of this planet and who remained on Earth to guide the budding civilization before Nibaru, and the other dark worlds polluted it. Your power is pure because it is intrinsic to your blood, your bones, and, most importantly, your DNA. Even so, the body you occupy is a physical body and is subject to this world's natural laws, limitations, and influences. Your mind is imprinted with the pattern of worldly thinking by the humans who surround you and have taught you how to think and act according to the human model of physical thought. Our goal tonight is to help you to clear away this past. Tonight, in accordance with God's Will, you will begin to know your true self, your true power, and the magnitude of your Hectaran heritage."

Before moving into new information, I summarized the pertinent information from *Volume One*, which all of the Weet had read. I then reminded them of the experiences they had had since we began to reconnect.

"When you were in your spirit form, you knew all of this," I continued. "You also knew that you would forget all of it when you came into your present bodies. You accepted that and also agreed to the return of your memories so that you could take up your duties as Strong Weet and apply your powers to the work of The Great Plan. The process of remembering is called 'Awakening' or 'Interfusion,' as Elise has named it. Your Awakening has begun, and we are here to support and guide you through the process."

Merta spoke up boldly, "What do you mean, 'we?' I am sorry to interrupt, but I need to know who you mean when you say, 'we are here to support you.' I know that *Pacha Mama* and many more as well are always with me. I thought that I, alone, was aware of them, but are these the same ones you speak of now."

I smiled at her and said, "Very good, Merta." Then I said to the whole group, "I want you all to sit quietly and observe."

Divine Energy suffused our bodies the way sunlight

permeates the leaves of a summer tree or the way the oceans and rivers feel when they meet. That is the best imagery I can come up with to describe the all-consuming, all-fulfilling contentment that streamed through each of us as we welcomed the silence.

"I can feel the energy of purity here," Sit said, speaking barely louder than a whisper. "I have never felt life force and love as strongly as I do at this moment." Her eyes glistened as she turned to Elise, who had put down her crocheting.

Elise looked at Sit and answered her unspoken question. "Yes, Sit. I see them, too."

"*Ai,* there are Saints here tonight," Merta said. "I am surprised, but I am not surprised, too." Then she looked around and frowned in puzzlement. "Where is *Pacha Mama?*"

"*Pacha Mama,* or Maria to those of you who do not know her, is very much with us, Merta," Elise responded. "She is taking a different form right now."

"Ah, yes. I am used to this behavior of hers. I understand now." Merta inhaled deeply and sat back more comfortably in her chair.

"What you have been experiencing is just a hint of the wealth of power. As the frequencies from Hectarus work to align your DNA, those powers will become increasingly available. You will soon be using the full scope of your strengths to fulfill your particular assignments within The Great Plan. Mother H and God developed The Great Plan eons ago to direct the dispersion of Unconditional Love and Truth throughout the Cosmos. Each of you has contributed to it for as long as you have been in existence. Your particular tasks will be made known to each of you sometime soon, as will the actions necessary to complete them. It will never be my job to teach you anything.

Everything you need to know comes from within you and from your receptivity to God working in your life. His Holy Spirit is always near to you.

"I will tell you this, however. You have a direct link to the elements of Nature, as do all of the Weet. Focusing on this Truth as you go about your daily activities will enhance your Awakening.

"We'll continue meeting once a month for a while, but as the frequencies increase in all of us, we'll come together more often. I think we've covered enough for now, so go home, rest, and do what you do. Feel free to email me if you have any questions or if anything out of the ordinary happens. I am so happy that we have been together tonight.

"Help yourself to some of Elise's jungle juice tea before you leave. She left a big jug of it in the kitchen."

"*Ai*," Merta cried. "That is not for me! I drink water only, please."

"We have plenty of that, Merta," I said. "Now, what do you all say we go fill our plates? Elise has worked hard on our dinner for this evening. When you fill your plates, come back in here. The other important reason we are all here tonight is to get to know one another better. And please don't feed the Poodles. They are getting fat."

"Oh, the babies!" Merta motioned to the Poodles. "Come here to Mama Merta. I love you, little babies. Kiss kiss."

"Oy vey!" I muttered as I rolled my eyes.

Daddy, be quiet. Don't even start.

ANNIE'S COSMIC ACTIVITY

Hi. Annie here. I had a free moment, so I thought I would take the opportunity to tell you a little more about myself. I hope you have immersed yourself enough in this book to have experienced some exciting changes in your life by now—changes that are key to determining the future of all life on Earth.

I want to give you all a little better explanation of who I am and tell you about some of the things I do that you cannot see with your physical eyes. Elise is writing this for me as the task is more suited to her particular frequencies than to Father's.

I am a pure Energy Being. I have no physical form, but everything I am made of comes directly from God. The energies of my Mother, Mary, fused with those of my Father, Din. I am the result of that union—a perfected Created Being. Because of my Father's love for me, I decided to take the form and shape of a teenage girl and maintain that image whenever I come to Earth. This is also the appearance I tend to use in most places throughout the universes and the one the Hectaran family is most familiar with seeing.

In the millions of years since my birth, I have helped my grandmother, known to you as Mother H, and Mother and Father to create, seed, and destroy civilizations throughout the universes. I have created planets and destroyed galaxies under Grandmother's instruction, who receives her direction from God, the Father of All.

I can go anywhere within the infinite boundaries of all the universes fueled by the essence of Unconditional Love within me and the power granted to me by God. I travel with ease in a manner that defies measurement by time, no matter how finely parsed, and is beyond understanding in this three-dimensional physical world.

I have often heard humans say, "Go with the flow." I like that. Although no human lives by it, it is an excellent attempt to describe what all beings are supposed to do. Humans on this planet have always been directed to place every aspect of life under God's Will. Every being in every part of all Universes was born to live in the flow of Unconditional Love and Truth and let those forces guide all thoughts, words, and deeds.

It is not complicated to live by the heart. It's just that the human world has been corrupted by greed, lust, anger, jealousy, hatred, and all things born within the human mind by ego. You were born into this world and raised by other humans influenced by that pollution and making choices affected by it. This has made it hard for beings to remember Who made them, but it is no excuse to stay trapped in the prison of your mind.

I have also come into a human body suit through Mother and Father—many times, in fact. I have lived through lifetimes where I, too, directly experienced the evil-doings of man, but I have always come to Earth knowing exactly who I am and what I am to do at that moment in Earth history to further the progress of The Great Plan.

We—the Family Triad that is—are dedicated to the task of overseeing the fulfillment of The Great Plan, and even though we are busier than ever now, it is not "all work and no play." I adore playing with the Elementals, Fire, Water, Air, Earth, and other Spirit Beings which your languages cannot describe and your three-dimensional plane cannot support. As I am one with everything in God's creation, I can fuse into the flames of Fire, cascade as Water, move as Air, and stream in and out of every particle of Earth. I also like to dance with the Northern Lights, swim with the dolphins, and make crop circles.

Earth began as a holy, shimmering orb of liquid light. Mother H meticulously crafted every detail before settling Earth's Spirit Being into its place in the Milky Way. She nursed it with her power and stitched the Earth's body into the web that she built for it, aligning it carefully to make it receptive to the resonance of the Creation Frequency.

The placement of Earth within the cosmos was a grand experiment perfectly ordained in thought by Mother H. It was to be a heaven-like place in the three-dimensional plane, colonized by Hectaran Beings, who would grow a civilization entirely devoted to God. When Mother H was satisfied with Earth's energy pattern and its secure link to the Creation Frequency, she converted the light body into a physical orb in this plane's material structure. The Spirit Beings that were born with the creation of Earth's energy pattern, including the Spirit of Earth herself, continue to exist on the physical Earth while retaining their connection to the other dimensions. Nowhere in the galaxy was there a new planet such as this beautiful new Earth. Her soils spoke with the Hum, the rocks whispered wisdom, and all elementals lived together joyously in preparation for the Hectaran Beings who would be SEEDED there to carry out God's Will.

I assisted with Earth's transformation to this physical realm by helping the Spirit Beings of Color and other star materials coordinate on Earth to combine and distribute the elements that comprise this planet. They came together in perfect harmony and aligned themselves in the embrace of the spirit of Earth, happy in the perfect completion of their task.

However, it was not long before the invasion of beings

from Nibaru, Sirius, and Orion forced Grandma to change her plans. The presence of these invaders with their ill will and intentions caused the landmass to recoil and shrink. But that was not all. Every element on the planet has a purpose and is needed to maintain the balance and well-being of the whole. Some of these elements are especially powerful and, with proper care, can be used for great good. Under the influence of the destructive thoughts from these invaders, humans used these elements to cause harm and destruction—sometimes from plain carelessness, but often from sheer malice.

Since then, one of my duties has been to check in with the various spirit beings and direct their activities to counteract the damage. Sometimes we tweak the chemistry a little, hide a uranium deposit, or reveal an alternative with an equal chance for good but less for ill. Sometimes it is necessary to cause an earthquake or release a volcano—like a doctor working on an ailing patient.

Mother H created Earth and its Spirit Being. Earth responds to abuses from humanity of her own will. I have spoken with her from time to time to avert disasters and cataclysms outside the parameters of The Great Plan. Earth is still the daughter of Mother H, and no human on the planet today knows her *true* essence. Whether or not humanity chooses to love and honor God, thereby convincing Mother H to let this world remain in existence, the Spirit Being of Earth will continue to thrive. Earth will be transfigured and transported to another dimensional space to heal, or she will be strengthened and cleansed by a higher dose of radiance from the Central Radiation Stone. The essence of the Spirit of Earth will not be harmed, for she is pure and straight from the mind of God. The cleansing of Earth involves only the Human species, which, as mentioned before, will be removed entirely if not enough of them return to God. Animals will, however, be allowed to repopulate the Earth, as they are and have always been pure in spirit.

I have other work to attend to now, but I will be back to share more to encourage your Awakening. Until then, keep your eyes on the stars. You never know when I might send up a brilliant display just for you. Remember, some of you reading this book may be Weet, and as such, you are related to me.

The Third Meeting of The Strong Weet

When I told Elise that I was planning to have the third meeting of the Strong Weet on November 1st, she reminded me that it is also *El Dia de los Muertos*, or All Saints' Day or All Souls' Day as it's known in English. Elise has celebrated that holy day in the Filipino style her whole life. Her Earth father was Filipino, and the observance of that day was filled with the rich and colorful traditions of the culture. The offerings of lit candles, marigolds, and sweets at the graves of deceased family members remind me of the practices and traditions found in the Catholic communities of the American Southwest and in the countries south of the border.

We agreed that the occasion would be an ideal time to share a little festivity. Still, I cautioned her not to get too carried away with the *El Dia de los Muertos* stuff, as everyone needed to be focused on the lessons and activities planned for the evening. I don't think she was really listening to me. I've noticed that she retains a strong attachment to certain aspects of Earth culture. That concerns me because she gets a bit immersed in it at times, and that could slow down her Awakening.

Needless to say, mention of that special day sent Elise running back to her house babbling about candles and Filipino desserts, and I think I heard something about marigolds on the coffee table.

The Day Before the Gathering

Father, you must do something for me.

Oh, Annie, don't I do everything for you? You're my favorite daughter.

Your only daughter.

Well, there's that. What do you want? Can't you see I'm busy getting ready for our meeting?

That's just it. This is not just a regular meeting. All Saints' Day is very important to Grandma and to God. You need to allow Elise to speak freely at certain times during the gathering tomorrow. She is the most experienced of the Strong Weet when it comes to speaking properly of the dead. Her Earth daddy just told me —

Is Pi here?

He's not here with us, but he's talking to me right now.

Hey, Pi.

As it turns out, Elise's Earth father, Pacelli, is also a strong Spirit Being who retained much of his awareness while in human form. Elise will be surprised when she finds out what he is doing, but that will come later. Wait, he's telling me things about El Dia de los Muertos now. Hold on.

A Minute or So Later

Okay, this is what Elise's Father just told me — oh, and Pi is his real spirit name. Even though this world's religions have done a poor job of properly honoring God, there are still some groups of people — Elise's daddy being one of them — who have pleased Grandma and God in their seasonal practices of devotion.

Here are Pi's exact words:

> *El Dia de los Muertos* is one of the more righteous traditions on this planet. Those who observe it are aware of the power of

communication with those who have left their bodies. As my daughter Elise can explain, when the people go to the gravesite on the night before All Saints' Day, there is only the silent offering of candles, sweets, and marigolds. When the morning comes, the people speak to the dead, sing the songs, and celebrate joyfully. These people have embraced the mystery of the afterlife while learning to combine Christ's teachings of unconditional love with genuine reverence for nature. Humans have maintained the observance of *El Dia de los Muertos* for centuries. Filipinos and others from similar cultures still go to the graves, leave the same flowers, and hold the same silence. As long as they remember to honor God and His Son, Jesus, while they recall and honor their ancestors, their actions can bring healing to all of humanity.

Thank you, Pi. So Father, don't dismiss whatever Elise has to offer tomorrow, okay? Even you still have a few things to learn.

As long as I can eat whatever sweets Elise brings over, anything she wants to do is fine by me.

That's really all I came to tell you. See you later.

And then she's gone. Just like her Mother.

Yes, dearest Din? Did you mention me?

Mary!

Do you require anything?

Well, no, I was just having a good time with Annie, but it's good to see you again. What's up?

Well, our Homeland is up.

You'll never get used to Earth expressions, will you? I

was just asking what's going on with you. What have you been doing? You still aren't saying much in this volume, are you?

I am saying more than anyone realizes. But one thing I am concerned about is something that does not seem to be connected with the meeting of the Strong Weet tomorrow. It has to do with El Dia de los Muertos. I want you to convey what I am about to say to the circle of the Strong Weet and include it in this volume as well.

Okay, this sounds big. What is it?

I am increasingly bothered by the language humans continue to use. Profanity on this planet is a sickness that grows with each year. We had hoped that the human species would have attained more significant intellectual development by now. Earth language is inadequate, to begin with, but when it becomes acceptable to sprinkle everyday conversation with foul words that mock and belittle God, it is an abomination. Even Elise needs to heed what I have to say, as she is subject to occasional slips in her own speech. I know this is a struggle for her, but it must cease. I do not want any of those words slipping out during a Development Circle when tender new Weet are present.

Because they allowed the darker beings to manipulate their DNA, Mother H deprived Earth beings of their natural ability to communicate by silent vibrations. Instead, humans were left to figure out how to vocalize sound patterns that could convey the basic requirements of life to the other members of their communities. Language became an indispensable tool that allowed people to live and work together for the benefit of all. It did not take long, however, for words to become a pathway to the imprisonment of their minds.

You are to instruct the Strong Weet to teach others the importance of eliminating foul words from their vocabulary. They must be aware that anything said contrary to the vibration of purity creates a dark, obstructing cloud in the speaker's spirit and in all others who hear the words. Of equal if not greater concern are the four-letter words and horrible slang phrases referring to mothers that teenagers and adults use. They are just plain insulting to Mother H, the Blessed Virgin Mary, and of course, God, Himself. I have been here on Earth often enough that I have come to expect the despicable behavior and speech of Earthlings. It is rampant and out of control. I don't let it get to me, but it does affect Mother. She is the one these people need to worry about as she is genuinely a Force to be reckoned with. The concern has nothing to do with religious morality or anything of the sort. It has to do with the intention of the heart and respect for God's children. The mouth projects what is in the heart and mind of a human being. If humans use words like these so frequently and so carelessly, what does that say about their true feelings for their Creator or each other? They may laugh at my warning now, but when they leave the body their Creator has given them, they will laugh no longer. I am here to tell everyone that whether you believe in a Creator God or not, it does not change the Truth that the Creator not only exists, but He is concerned with all the affairs of humanity. Profanity separates humankind from God, while devotion draws people closer. Devotion to God is the key to saving this world from annihilation.

Mary, did I just hear you say, "I don't let it get to me," to state that something doesn't bother you? That's a modern Earth phrase.

Well, I must have picked it up from you. I'm going to stop speaking now, Din.

Ego and Humanity's Need to Return to God

There's still a little time before the Development Circle starts, so I've asked Elise to jot down some thoughts about another important matter. As I have mentioned before, many human characteristics and activities interfere with and damage the Creation Frequency. The thing that drives these behaviors to dangerous levels is ego. Without ego, they would either stop or be turned to useful and benevolent purposes. The ego is perhaps the biggest problem of all, leading to the demise of humanity.

From the Writings of Elise

This is a vast topic, but here goes. I write not just for the benefit of the readers but so that I, too, might feel the relief of God's medicine in my own struggle with ego.

The most critical need on the planet right now is for the collective detachment from ego. This must happen individually to affect the whole. There is no way around it. There is no communal prayer that will get humanity out of the mess it has created for itself. Every single person on this planet needs to look first up to the stars and then begin their own release. The release will coincide with the return to God.

Herein lies the irony: We must use our own faculties, mental and physical, to supersede our egos. Why? Because we live in limited, three-dimensional bodies. The mental cleansing process must begin immediately, and you must stick with it. It is easier than it might seem. It just takes the decision to do it. Once you make a genuine effort and conscious decision to do this, you will receive more assistance from the cosmos than you can possibly imagine. Starting right here, right now.

The intentional removal of what I call "brain garbage," may be accompanied by some discomfort. The energy of ego does not want you to realize that it is a force foreign to your being. Ego requires that you stay trapped in your own mental wanderings, believing that you have always been disconnected from God or possibly that God never even existed. We must acknowledge that we have kept ourselves trapped in our love affair with personal identity—ego.

You are a prisoner and a slave. You want freedom? Then make yourself laugh. Go to the mirror, stick your tongue out, and put your finger up your nose.

Feel better now?

***

In my own dealings with the ego that used to consume every part of my existence, I realized that I could make things a lot easier if I intentionally did things to make myself laugh. I saw for myself that everything I thought concerning the sadness of such and such past story, or my anger at so-and-so for how they treated me, et cetera, was just the dusted energy of the past and had nothing to do with me or my relationship to God. In fact, every time I radiated rage or wept despondently, I blocked the flow of infinite cosmic streams of power I would otherwise receive. It is absolutely *incorrect* to say that God cuts off Love—God IS Love—or severs communication to or from anyone. Instead, it is by one's own will and choice that any individual can be a receptacle for the bountiful rays of Love God sends them.

Remember the words of Mary at the end of *Volume One*:

> Earth ... will be shunned and forgot-
> ten ... It will be as if it never existed,
> and all of the Spirits of those who lived
> here will be forever terminated.

So, what can be done to assist in this most arduous of tasks? The best thing is to find the time to welcome complete silence. I do not mean silence maintained in meditation, or that you need to assume any particular posture, or that you need any tools to help you achieve silence. The only thing necessary is to shut out any and all noise. Silence is the best way to receive the heart. Silence is the ultimate form of prayer, and in joining it, one acknowledges the intention to commune with God. This is not to say that worded prayers are wrong or ineffective, for there are ancient prayers whose frequencies are well-fitted to the purpose of spiritual control of the ego. For humans, however, the most effective form of prayer is to stop all noise, externally and internally. Total silence is perfect prayer.

It may also be beneficial to record the progress of your own Interfusion by keeping a journal, if you are so inclined. If you do, be careful that you don't become attached to and enthralled by your own thoughts. That is a trap your ego enjoys immensely. Writing incessantly about feelings and describing the details of your daily experiences can serve to feed the ego.

The key is to keep it simple. Practice undoing your thoughts with laughter. Practice in silence, even if for just two minutes. Do something easy, free, and fun. Do not dwell on the past. It does not exist. Living in the past is a waste of precious energy that would be better used to create a bright, new future for you and those you love.

Elise Tells about the Meeting in the Park

I could hardly contain my glee when Din told me that we would be holding our third Development Circle in the nearby state park. I'm really looking forward to being outside under the sun and sky.

I pulled into the parking lot at the trail head and saw Din's car parked near my favorite Oak tree. We greeted each other then walked over to the edge of the creek to wait for Merta and Sit. We could keep an eye on the parking lot from there, and it was certainly more pleasant than standing around on the asphalt.

The patches of stinging nettle along the side of the trail were beginning to die down for the season. I picked one of the last green leaves from a nearby plant and ate it. The act reminded me of how little time I had spent gathering herbs this season compared to previous years.

"What are you doing? You're going to make a hole in your throat with that," Din said, laughing as he watched me chew the nettle leaf.

"Nettle can be eaten fresh when the leaves are young and green but are best gathered for tea when they are larger. Do you see that green seed-looking thing in the middle of the plant? That's the fruit, which tells you that this plant does not want to be picked anymore. That is its baby and indicates that the whole plant has turned toxic." I was beginning to feel a burning sensation in my mouth, but I wasn't about to let Din know.

"So why did you eat it?" Din asked with a smirk.

"One would have to consume at least five leaves to have a noxious effect. I've always tested the edible plants a little at a time to get to know them as well as possible. You should get to know the planet you live on a little better," I said lightly, then walked on.

Din took a deep breath and shook his head.

The sun shone brilliant and pure, and a gentle fall breeze rustled the colorful leaves that still clung to the tree branches. A large deer and her fawn stepped out of the shadows about thirty feet away from us.

We stood still, as did the two wild Beings. Their sleek brown bodies complemented the carpet of lovely autumn colors on the ground beneath us. The mother's black eyes glistened with her own inner light, and I could feel the concern she radiated at the sight of two humans so near her baby.

The fawn stepped closer to us. I felt the mother's anxiety increase, but then she seemed to relax and let her baby move closer. I dared not move a muscle.

The fawn continued its movement toward us — twenty-five feet, then twenty feet. My heart swelled with such joy that I forced myself to breathe deeper to stay calm and not disturb the two deer in any way. I felt my radiance merge with the radiance of these precious creatures, which allowed them to observe my GLOW and feel more comfortable with me. I did nothing physical except to remain still and pay attention to my breath.

Din had to explain to me later what happened next because my recall ends at that point. The fawn walked right up to me, nuzzled its face into my arm and hip, and then trotted back to its mother. The pair of them turned and slipped silently back into the shadows.

"What? How did that happen with me not knowing it?" It annoyed me that, for some reason, I had temporarily lost consciousness.

Din looked at me and laughed. "It's so funny to watch how it's all returning to you, Elise," he said. "You tell me. Why did you 'tune out'?"

"Well, when the fawn started to approach me, I began to feel myself slip away. I felt like I was turning into something totally connected with the baby and its mama. Then suddenly, I was gone. I think that in some strange way, I *became* that doe."

"It's time you acknowledge that you are in complete union with all animal spirits on this planet, don't you think?"

"Wow. That's beautiful but still a little hazy. Does that mean that I could tame a wild tiger if I wanted to? Could I make all the ticks decide to eat themselves? Or, better yet, convince the mosquitoes that their new food of choice is not the blood of mammals but the blood of ticks?"

"Don't get ahead of yourself," Din said. "Enjoy what just happened and come back to the experience later. You were given a wonderful gift just now."

"I guess that explains all my childhood thoughts of turning into dolphins, fish, and turtles. I knew it was happening, just not this three-dimensional reality. What good is it to have powers like unity with animal Spirits if you can't see the effect? Where's the fun in that? I'm not going to commit suicide or anything, but I have often thought of the beauty of getting off this world."

A woman's voice bright with laughter called through the woods like a bird's song. "Oh, *mija*, please don't do that! We would miss your jungle juice."

Din and I looked and saw Merta and Sit coming down the trail, each with a big grin on her face.

"Or if you do decide to go, figure out a way to take us with you," Sit said, laughing.

"What a wonderful day to be gathering together, huh?" Sit said merrily. "It's good to see you all again."

"Sure is," Din said. "Now, let's find a spot and get down to business."

We walked down the trail to the entrance to the cave. I suggested we go down into it, as there were enough large rocks for us all to sit comfortably. It's chilly inside the cave, but everyone was prepared for colder air as the weather here can be unpredictable this time of year.

We were greeted by the sound of the rushing water but there were plenty of dry rocks for us to sit on. The cave's acoustics amplified Din's voice and caused it to resonate in the enclosed space. Somehow he seemed to grow and expand as the words flowed from him. The lighting in the cave was dim, and I could see a strange illumination around the heads of Din, Merta, and Sit, each one a different, vibrating color.

"Din, you're looking mighty Golden today," I said. "And Merta, you are as Rosy as ever. Sit, that's a lovely Aquamarine halo you're wearing."

"Well, Elise, can you see yourself?" Din said. "I see a Purple-Bluish ball where you're sitting."

The air rippled with our laughter, and I had an unusual sensation that seemed to indicate that the cave was happy we were all there.

"We are all nicely in tune with our GLOWS, and that is what I like to hear, Weet," Din said as we all settled down again. "I also want to hear how about your progress on the assignment I gave last time we met. Merta, how are you coming along in your nature work?"

"Well, I work in my gardens every day, and I have become used to something that most people would consider abnormal."

Sit smiled and nodded knowingly. "I bet I know what

you're talking about," she said.

"Well, the *chiquitos* talk to me through the flowers, the trees, and even the grasses. The small ones speak to me so much that it's hard to keep all of their messages straight. I have learned, especially in the past few weeks, that I don't need to even think anything in response. It's like they understand what I want to share with them, with me doing nothing at all. This is the only new thing, as I used to use thoughts that came like words in my head and sometimes even speak out loud to them. Now that just gets in the way. I like the do-nothing way of communicating with them much better.

"Oh, yes, I am also a little worried because *Pacha Mama* has not come to visit me in a very long time, and Burro has been acting just like the dog that he is, with no sign of *Pacha Mama* in him. She won't even appear when I call to her. This is not good to me."

"Don't worry, Merta," I said. "You know she is in *en forma de espíritu, si*? She could be very busy with some particular assignment from God. The universes are very big.

"*Si*, but I am just so used to her being with me so much of the time. I guess that's all for now."

"Merta, I want you to continue with your silent communication," Din said encouragingly. "You have just shared with us a critical power that is exclusive to the Strong Weet, and that is your awareness of communication with the nature spirits. Your assignment is to work on recognizing the different Spirit Beings in your garden. Get to know them individually, and the next time we gather, you can tell us about the different frequencies each of them emits. Is that clear?"

It was clear that Din was already aware of everything Merta had shared. He spoke as if he was running through a checklist of information that someone had given him.

Din turned his attention to Sit and said, "Now, Sit, tell us what has been going on in your life, nature-wise, since we last met."

"Do you have a couple of hours? Something extraordinary has happened almost every day since you gave us our first assignment to work with the elements. Merta, I'm a devoted gardener, too, and the flowers, trees, and plants that I tend are my dearest friends. I have spent my adult life studying each of them in minute detail. I have always had a passionate curiosity about the botanical world, and I have tried to learn about as much of it as possible.

"Since our last meeting, I have actually been communing with some of the botanicals in ways that, at first, were a little disturbing, but only because it was brand new. Or so it seemed at the time."

Sit was quiet for a moment and then continued, "You people here are the only ones I can share this with. Everyone else in the world would think I am crazy.

She paused again, and Din gave her a nod of encouragement. "Go on," he said.

Sit took a deep breath, and started to tell her story. "I have actually entered every flower growing in my garden. I mean, I have experienced a kind of direct merging with the interior structures of the flowers, leaves, stems, seeds, and roots of each plant. At first, it was visual. I simply saw the walls, membranes, chloroplasts, and other organelles of each cell—like looking through a microscope. At first, I thought I was hallucinating. I went inside and took my temperature just to rule out that possibility, but it was normal. The experience was so extraordinary, but it was also great fun. I went back to the gardens again and again, to various plants to see how they differed and how they were the same."

"This is wonderful. What happened?" I exclaimed,

unable to hide my enthusiasm.

"Again, when this all first started I was merely an observer looking on from the outside. Lately, though, I find myself pulled inside, like that ride at Disneyland makes you feel as if you've been shrunk down smaller than an atom. Now I see everything from the inside out. I don't see just a plant's structures either—which is amazing in itself. I can see what the plant is actually made of and what holds it together—pure light. I certainly did not learn to see things this way when I was in college, but my training and experience as a scientist have left my mind open to all sorts of possibilities. These sessions in the garden are wonderful, and I look forward to more explorations. Also, although I have never been inclined toward the production of two-dimensional art, I've been playing around with colored pencils and markers to try to more accurately convey what I am seeing. Words alone are inadequate.

"That's wonderful, Sit," Din said. "I'd love to see your drawings sometime."

Then he turned his attention to me. "I don't need to ask you what you've been up to lately, Elise. I just witnessed your ability to communicate with animal spirits. Why don't you tell Merta and Sit what went on between you and the doe and her fawn."

I took a moment before speaking to reflect on that event. In a flash of memory, I realized that I had not lost consciousness in the usual sense. Instead, my awareness had expanded and merged with that of the fawn, its mother, and all deer everywhere throughout time. I began to share the story of the deer with the group.

"There is no separation between myself and every other living Being, animal or plant, on this planet," I said as I wrapped up my story. "I am only beginning to recall what that is all about. My experience today with the little fawn and its mother was a gift to help me understand. That is really all I have to say—oh, and thank you, God."

We sat for a while without talking, knowing that the rushing water was all we were meant to hear. The flow of the water seemed to foreshadow the flow of the events yet to come our way.

I felt Mother H's presence with us as a powerful embrace. It filled me with warmth and surrounded me with comfort. It seemed to convey the happiness she felt with our acceptance of the return of our gifts.

The gathering had been short, but Din felt our purpose had been met. He suggested we leave the cave for a short hike along the trail before we went our separate ways. There was no discussion of the next meeting.

ELISE REVEALS THE TOOLS OF THE WEET

A tool is any object, often handheld, that is used to carry out a particular task. The word is derived from "tol," an Old English word meaning "to prepare." Humans use tools in virtually every aspect of their lives, from simple sticks to find grubs to eat or make holes to plant seeds, to modern computers to make complex calculations, analyze data, or simply communicate rapidly over great distances.

The tools used on this planet are physical and operate within the parameters of this three-dimensional realm where humans have focused most of their awareness. There is, however, an array of powerful cosmic tools available to those who know how to operate beyond the physical realm. The actual instruments of the Strong Weet cannot be described or defined by anything within human understanding. The power coursing through a Strong Weet is pure and of such force that no physical object, be it wand, crystal, herb, candle, incense, et cetera, has the strength to manipulate or control it, nor can it be invoked by prayer or incantation. A Strong Weet has no use for such devices but understands how they have found their place among humanity in this dimension.

The energy frequencies used to perform "magic" are generated by a connection to God and the power of pure Thought. "Thought" is a cosmic gift and is the principal tool used by a Strong Weet. This Thought, however, is not the ordinary string of mental imagery that originates from the physical, conscious mind. It is the vibration generated by the Spirit of God in the synapses of the Strong Weet and emerges coherent and understandable in the conscious human mind.

True magic—science that has not yet been discovered on this world—requires the ability to become empty enough to receive the stream of direct messages and commands from the Spirit Beings of Hectarus. There must also, of course, be the ability to interpret the messages and respond to them appropriately. True magic is a tool used to communicate the need for specific actions and to bring them about as requested by a Higher Being, Mother H, or the Creator.

A Strong Weet's ability to communicate with the Elemental Spirit Beings is often called upon to fulfill a request from Mother H. She may deem it necessary to cause an immediate downpour of rain, for instance. Mother H may call on a Strong Weet to work with the Spirit of Air and Sky to bring it about. The Strong Weet does not know why the storm is needed, but only that Mother commands it and should not be questioned. Mother H often delegates tasks to other capable beings. The Strong Weet are and have always been the Hectaran Beings who do much of the actual work in the three-dimensional realm of Earth.

The Spirit Beings of Hectarus who are active on Earth are too numerous to count. Air, sun, birds, plants, fire, water, fish, and four-legged creatures are just some of the forms they occupy that are apparent to the eyes of the world. They assist with the stewardship of Earth—a task that has become more demanding as much of humanity has forgotten its commission to be caretakers and guardians. A myriad of other invisible Spirit Beings exists who have never taken form and have been the inspiration for much of what appears in human mythologies, folklore, and fairy tales. This combined family of Spirit Beings remains present and active on Earth, ready to assist the Strong Weet in their work.

We must never forget the great Spirit Beings, some of whom once walked in bodies on Earth. Some of these Beings are well-known to humans, but many more lived their lives on Earth anonymously. Their lives, teachings, and devotional work have positively impacted The Great Plan, even though much of it has been forgotten by most humans.

Messages are transferred from the ancestral realm as well. All the grandmothers and grandfathers who have walked in your family line can communicate with you. Everything True and of Unconditional Love comes directly from God. Visions or dreams of a long-deceased great-aunt or grandfather speaking or presenting a gift are real. They are all waiting for their descendants to respond to them with the same energetic frequency they use to reach them.

Life becomes truly powerful and purposeful with the devoted practice of unconditional Love. Your birthright is to be happy, but not because of anything that the world or your conscious mind has done for you. Find the place in the nothingness inside you. Use any tool, physical or spiritual, as necessary, but always be aware of the tool's origin and its true purpose.

DIN RELATES AN OCCURRENCE IN THE LIFE OF MERTA

I do not believe that anything affecting the lives of the Strong Weet is random or coincidental. Everything is for a purpose and can be a lesson for those who may wonder about their own relationship to God or, perhaps, the possibility that they might be one of the as-yet-undiscovered Weet. To that end, I have asked Merta for permission to share the details of a recent profound and tragic event in her life.

***

I received the following email from Merta a few days ago:

> I must meet with you, Din. I am
> not sure I can continue.

The message was a complete surprise as Merta rarely uses the computer to communicate. I was greatly alarmed and concerned, so I dropped everything to find my phone to call her. I had no idea what was going on, and my anxiety was increased as neither Annie nor Mother was around to fill me in.

Merta picked up her phone on the second ring. I barely understood what she was saying between sobs.

"Hello, Merta? It's me, Din. Are you okay? What's going on? I just now got your email."

"*Ai. O, Dios, por qué? Por qué? Madre, por favor*

173

ayúdame. Please help me." Merta cried uncontrollably between her frantic words.

I waited a moment and then said, "Merta. It's me, Din. Take a deep breath, and tell me, are you safe? Do you need help?"

Her dog whimpered in the background, and I heard her blow her nose. I had no clue what was going on, but I was concerned for Merta's safety. She's a tiny lady who lives by herself and a Strong Weet whose well-being I was responsible for.

"I am okay. It's my son, Marco. He's gone. He's gone. *Ai, Dios. Mi hijo esta muerto.*" Merta began to wail.

"Merta, I am coming to your house right now. You stay right where you are and don't call anyone else. I will be there as fast as I can." I hung up the phone, thankful that I had her address in one of my notepads. I grabbed my coat and keys and drove to Merta's house fast enough to turn the twenty-minute trip into one of only twelve.

I heard her still crying as I knocked on her front door. It took her nearly five minutes to respond. Her face was red, and tears streamed from her eyes. She started to collapse as I entered. I caught her before she fell, eased her gently to the floor, and closed the door behind me.

My heart went out to the little woman seated on the floor moaning in misery. I squatted down beside her and placed my hand on her forehead. "Merta, Merta, I'm here. It's Din," I said. "Tell me what has happened."

She looked up at me and said, "My son, Marco, has been killed. I have lost my only son."

"Oh, Merta, I am so sorry. So sorry." There is really nothing that can be said to truly help a person in such a state, so I chose silence.

She got up slowly, using my arm for support, and looked at me. "Marco was the only reason I had left down here," she said. "Now, there is nothing. All my family is gone. There is nothing more to be done."

I encouraged her to sit down in her reading chair. There was a teacup on the table next to the chair. I picked it up and felt that it was still warm then placed it into her hands.

She sipped absent-mindedly before speaking. "He was killed in an automobile accident. A drunk driver smashed into him at an intersection yesterday, but I was not told until today."

Burro nuzzled up next to her feet, and I scratched his ears while Merta continued, "The police said that Marco's body was so badly smashed in the wreckage that they could not find any information about him at first. They could see his license plate number, but it took them a while to find his wallet in the mess where they finally found my name and number. They said there is no point in me coming to see the body because he is unrecognizable in the face. *Ai,* my heart is ripping, Din. I don't know why this happened to my Marco. He was such a pure man. He was so good. This is all wrong, *Dios*. All wrong!"

Merta pounded her fist against the armrest of her chair, causing the lamp on the side table to shake.

"There are so many evil people in this world, and I have lost so many of my family already. You cannot know what it is like to lose your only child, Din. You cannot know what this feels like." She looked at me with immense sadness, tears spilling from her eyes.

I didn't tell her then, but I actually do know what it's like to lose a beloved child. In fact, I have experienced the loss of many dear family members from the many lives I have lived, but I left that thought unsaid. For that moment, the best I could offer was my silence.

Merta took another sip of tea and said, "I have chosen not to go to where they have his remains. I know he is not there. I am arranging for the burial and will go to the city where he lived to escort the body back home. He grew up in this house." She looked around the room. "He grew up in this house," she repeated softly, then turned her agonized gaze back to me and said, "This is all so much, Din. I don't know what is going on right now. Where is *Pacha Mama*?"

Aqui, mija, aqui. Estoy aqui, Merta.

The two of us looked up and saw *Pacha Mama* standing in front of us in the living room. I was not surprised to see her as I know full well who she is, but I could tell that Merta was slightly shocked.

Hola, Din.

I inclined my head in greeting and remained quiet. It was not for me to speak.

Merta, I want you to know that Marco is with me. He is fine, and you must calm down now and listen to me. It is good, Din, that you have come to Merta's side.

Merta looked at me then turned her gaze back to *Pacha Mama*.

"Where is my Marco? I want to speak with him."

Calme, Merta. You must control yourself. Feel me, mija.

At that moment, a wave of Blue washed over us, penetrating and lifting our spirits with solace and peace. *Pacha Mama* came forward and stroked Merta's brow.

Marco is with Jesus, el Christo, Merta. The Blessed Virgin Mary is also with him. He is right where he needs to be, but he cannot speak with you right now. He wants me to tell you that he loves you and hopes you will be calm enough to understand why this has happened. Our Marco is such a dear, dear heart. I need to explain to you why he has left the Earth so suddenly.

Pacha Mama — or Mary, as I know her — looked at me and smiled. I smiled back, knowing what she was about to say.

You know how truly special and devoted our Marco was to you and God on Earth, Merta. He was such a good little boy, a perfect child, and he always treated you with respect, obedience, and love. Is this not so, Merta?

"*Si.* He was a perfect child of God. My Marco, my only son."

You need to understand that he became aware of your true nature quite some time ago, even before you did. He knew that it was his job to continue to watch you, even though he was told to move to a different city. Our Marco is very strong, mija, and he did his job here perfectly.

Burro nuzzled up closer to Merta, nearly lying on top of her feet.

You don't remember this now, but you will. Marco chose to leave the Earth in this way so that he could help you, Merta.

"What? To help me? This is not helping me. This is destroying me, *Pacha Mama.* I don't understand." Merta clutched the cross she wore on a chain around her neck and took a deep breath. "*Ai,* but I do," she said. "*Ai, Christo, Madre, me ayuda.* Please help this to be clearer now."

Marco knew that you are a very special Being, Merta. He has always known that you are a Strong Weet, and he knew of the important work that you have always done and that you need to finish down here. He knew there would come a time in your lives when he would be able to help you regain your knowledge of this so that you could assist with The Great Plan of God. He knew that by his actions and choices, he could help you to return to your knowing much sooner. We did not know how he would help you, but now we can see.

"What do you mean, 'now we can see'? All I can see is that my only beloved son has left his body and is gone from my eyes. My only son."

Merta. Merta. Breathe. Feel Marco's love for you.

As Merta closed her eyes, I saw the color around her head change from Grey to Pink and Gold. She still clutched her cross.

"*Oh, mi Dios.* My blessed boy left so that he could help me come back to my Spirit Being quicker. He chose to leave suddenly so that I would embrace the work I agreed to do so long ago, for The Great Plan. Oh, *mi Marco, mi Marco.* This is so beautiful, but it is still so very painful, *Pacha Mama.*"

Do you see what is around you, Merta? Open your eyes.

A whole host of Beings had joined us in the room, all of them Hectaran, all of them meaningful to Merta's lives on Earth and to her true life back home. A shower of White light fell through the ceiling, and we stood in the midst of it. The pure light of Hectarus showered down into Merta's living room for her. The sensation was like nothing even I had ever felt before. It was as if everything in the world had disappeared, and there was nothing on Earth at that moment but Hectarus. I glanced at Merta, whose face was suffused with radiant Rose light so that I could barely make out its actual shape and form. I saw her in her true Spirit Being form.

"*Ai,* I will never doubt the Holy One's actions in this life ever again. *Gracias, Marco. Gracias, Dios.*" Merta sniffed, looked up to the ceiling, and smiled. "My only question is how will I ever again be content to live in this world after what I have just seen?"

I smiled, and Burro thumped his tail happily on the floor at Merta's feet.

Elise's Trip to Monk's Mound

Hearing Din's report about what happened to Merta's son brought back my own memory of how I felt upon learning of the death of a loved one.

***

I was riding my bicycle across the commons area of the college I attended when a twisting, wrenching pain stabbed through my gut and caused me to fall. I think a few people came to assist me, but I didn't really notice because of the tremendous pain that swept through my belly. The pain passed nearly as soon as it came upon me, leaving behind the awareness that my father, Pacelli — or Pi as he was known to his family — had left his body.

At the time, I used the word "dead" to describe his state of being. I know now that is not correct, as there is no such thing as death — at least not in that sense.

I got back on my bike and rode back to the house I shared with my boyfriend at the time. He looked distraught when he greeted me at the door and immediately came over and hugged me. He stepped back so he could look into my eyes. Keeping his hands on my shoulders, he said, "Your sister called, Elise."

"Yes, I know. My dad is dead."

"How did you know? She said she hadn't talked to you yet,"

"Either Dad or something else out there wanted me to know. A bolt of energy stabbed through my stomach while I was riding home from school. Whatever it was certainly wanted me to know right then because the pain

179

of it knocked me right off my bike. I was going pretty fast, too."

"You don't seem too sad about it," he said.

"Well, he had a heart condition, so I knew it was coming. I may get stupid about a lot of things in life, mostly because of my own opinions, but death is just one of those things that I don't waste too much time on. Personally, I'll be glad to be finished with my body down here—" I broke off when I saw the confusion and disbelief growing on his face.

"Um … okay, then. Your sister said the funeral is in two days. I'll go with you if you want."

"We'll see," I said as I went into the bedroom and closed the door.

***

That happened almost exactly twelve years ago. In retrospect, my reaction seems cold-hearted and callous. The truth is that I spoke honestly and acted to protect myself. Occupation of a human form subjects one to a confusing array of mental constructs that lure the individual into behaving in certain predictable ways. I have always struggled with this.

Everyone has their own particular coping mechanisms to deal with the passage of loved ones. Mine became a recipe for disaster. My attitude on the surface was cavalier. I said things like, "I know that it was just his body," and "My dad is still around," The glimmer of my spirit tried to speak to me, but my conscious mind was leading me downward fast.

I was raised in a Filipino family whose culture is absorbed in Catholic religiosity. We are taught from an early age that heaven is real, that sins affect what ultimately happens to a person, and that there is only one God. This background was not enough to make Pi's passing easy for me by any means. I was caught up in all things ego even though I knew that all people are not merely their bodies or minds. My mind was devoted to the illusion of the past and not to the heart-felt present or future.

I nearly killed myself during the next two years by starving my body. I internalized all the unresolved issues of my painful childhood with my father, and I didn't realize what that was doing to my body, let alone my mind. I am five-foot-ten, and my weight dropped to ninety-six pounds. It took three months of forced hospitalization to get me back on track. In the process, I discovered that an individual's worst enemy is a mental construct of their own creation.

At Monks Mound

To commemorate the anniversary of my father's passing, I took my children to Cahokia Mounds, just east of St. Louis, Missouri, for the first time. Pi was the one who took me for my first visit to this sacred area where the Cahokia civilization flourished for nearly five hundred years beside the Mississippi River. I knew something called me to be there that day, but I did not know that the visit was to entail so much more.

A feature known as Monks Mound, a one-hundred-foot-tall terraced earthwork constructed almost two thousand years ago, dominates the site. The city, whose original name is lost in history but is now known as "Cahokia," waxed and waned for about seven hundred years. It experienced a period of exceptional peace and prosperity that lasted about one hundred and fifty years during that time. This "golden age" coincided with the completion of the great mound. Their leader, the Sun Chief, established his residence and temple on the broad, flat top of the mound. This High Priest and principal leader of Cahokia was strongly connected to the Great Spirit and possessed great spiritual wisdom. The religious structure of Cahokia included ranks of priests whose primary occupation was to map the movements of the celestial bodies. Acting on their reports, the Sun Chief interceded on behalf of the people by offering prayers from the temple at the top of the mound appropriate to the time and season, and led the people in worship and celebration on days of significance such as equinoxes and solstices. These observances acknowledged and honored the sun as a gift directly from God and maintained the health, unity, and prosperity of the people.

Cahokia was the center of religious and spiritual observance and learning for the region. The people who lived there flourished because of it, and the city became a center of commerce, agriculture, and culture. As all things of the earth are also of the spirit, the strong link between the worldly and spiritual components of their society gave the Cahokia people their true wealth — the knowledge and wisdom of a multitude of foods, animals, earthen creations, dress adornment, tools, and, of the highest value, stories. Each of these gifts reflected Creator in its unique way, and trading them was another act of devotion and learning.

Stories held great value for these people whose history was known and shared only through the spoken word. They believed that Creator could be "seen" in the vibratory patterns of speech and, therefore, considered all spoken words to be an act of the Creator. The citizens and priests committed to preserving and sharing stories were individuals of great power as they directly represented Truth coming from God. No one among the Cahokians knew all of the stories in their entirety. Some people carried stories of plants and the rituals of their growth and harvest. Others told the stories of fire, air, water, and the stars. Some people even told stories about mundane things such as how and why clay pots are made. Everything in life had a story that informed the people of its history and purpose.

In the beginning, this world and everything in it was spoken into existence by God. The words He used were carried forth by energetic frequencies with tremendous generative power. In other words, God told a Story, and the world took shape. The stories told by the people of Cahokia generate similar frequencies that harmonize with the original Frequency to strengthen and maintain Creation and all life that springs from it. These people and others of similar traditions throughout history and around the world were fully aware of how important it was that every aspect of their lives should reflect their devotion to God. They lived by Truth.

***

The day was warm but windy and overcast. Rain had been in the forecast for St. Louis, so as I drove eastward, I prayed silently, asking God to hold back the rain until we completed our visit. I felt something special would happen and wondered if it might be connected to my father's spirit.

My daughter and I climbed to the top of the giant mound. When we reached the broad open terrace, a penetrating heat filled my body, and my little daughter danced around me. She must have felt something of what I felt as she exclaimed joyfully, "We are supposed to do something very special here, Mommy!"

I appreciated her natural exuberance, but I instructed her to remain quiet and to stay by my side, wherever I was.

She readily obeyed when I reminded her of the status and responsibilities of the person who had lived there. I was happy that she was there with me atop Monk's Mound, and knew that her energy had been called to be there alongside mine.

We walked to the eastern edge of the terrace, where I squatted down and placed my hands flat on the dirt between clumps of grass. I wanted first to honor God, then my Earth father, Pi, and then all Sun Chiefs who had ever lived upon this Mound.

"I am here, Blessed One, Great Mystery of All, to honor the Fathers and all the work they did for the people and for You, Holy One, while they dwelt here. I am aware that this creation was your home, Fathers, and I come with only my heart to offer. Please reach me in this moment, as there is something more that I must do, and I need your guidance to do it now, for this place. In the Love of Wakan Tanka, I touch this mound, touching you all."

I felt tingles shoot up and down my spine like streams of liquid fire, then I heard, *"Offer now, your body, child."*

Puzzled, I said, "Father? Do you want me to cut my finger to drop some blood here? Or maybe I can find a way to cut some of my hair."

"Offer now, your body, child. Let your words be as the water for us."

Then I understood. I used my finger to dig three small holes in the dirt marking out a triangle, and spat into each hole. As the saliva dripped from my mouth, I was aware of words in a strange and beautiful language spilling out with it and into the dry earth of the ancient sacred mound. My essence, my prayer, my body-being flowed into the mound, as had been the intention of whomever had drawn me to the site.

My awareness rose above my body as the words soaked

into the dirt, and I watched the light energy of my prayer enter the Mound with them. They appeared to me as an effervescent White light as they traveled down through the earth. Upon reaching the core of the mound, they exploded like a supernova with a Golden hue found nowhere else, not even the sun. I watched my body fizzle into the blast, pulled downward and upward at the same time. Next, an orchestra of vivid colors fanned out like the tail of a male peacock strutting his stuff. Heavenly Blues, Greens, Pinks, shades of Rose, Gold, Orange, Purple, Silver, White—all looping and streaming into, out of, and around the mound.

I returned to my body filled with awe. I looked around and saw my daughter squatting next to me. She was gazing up at the sky, mesmerized. I stood up and motioned for her to follow me. We walked to the southern edge of the terrace overlooking the side where the steps lead to the top. We were still alone, but I could see a few people on the plain below us. They looked like ants from our perspective, and they all seemed to be walking away from the mound. I thanked God for preserving the solitude for the necessary work of that moment.

We squatted at the edge of the mound, and, once again, I heard the voice issue a firm, steady command, *"Feel my Fire, Daughter. Speak as the Medicine. Give this as the ones of the plants give. Use this in thy words upon the trees."*

This time, I understood the meaning without asking for clarification. Purple Blue flames shot through my head from the base of my brain, and I saw nothing but that fire coming from my head, mouth, and hands. I stood up and lifted my hands to the sky. The sun burned through the layer of clouds and breathed deeply of the Purple Blue. I looked up and saw a Red-tailed Hawk soaring overhead in circles. It was big, but each circuit brought it lower until it was only about twenty feet above us. It was then that I could see how truly huge it was. Its tail feathers glowed Red against the backlight of the sun, and I marveled at its beauty. I have never seen one so big, so bright, and so close. The wonders of God spilled over everything and consumed us. I have never been happier in all of my days as I was in those moments.

We moved to the western edge of the mound, where we were instructed to remain standing. Again, I heard a voice. This time, it was feminine, and I knew at once whose powerful voice it was.

"It shall all be washed away if there is no return to the love of God."

I saw torrential floods pull down skyscrapers. I saw the spirit of Water mix with Fire and cosmic light to purify the planet. Nothing was left. I heard the fury of the Water and witnessed the holy cleansing it brought. I knew that Mother H directed all of this with her shifting gaze from where she stood above the raging elements. The cataclysm engulfed the whole world and then — nothing. I saw nothing but a dark space where the planet Earth once breathed. The sun changed course, and its rays, no longer needed for Earth's sustenance, gathered into a new mass. I watched the Golden web that had surrounded Earth darken and disintegrate and the portal that connected it to the rest of the universe close and disappear. I looked upon the most empty and lonely point in space. I saw clearly one possible future for this world.

Then I saw Mother H standing before us, her arms open wide in invitation. I took hold of my daughter's hand, and we walked toward her. Before we knew it, we were wrapped in Mother H's embrace and floating through the air. She set us down gently at the northern edge of the mound where we remained standing. Without prompting, I offered my own prayer to the Originating Mystery of the Lakota Sioux:

> Wakan Tanka, for all that has been shown
> now, and all that I have offered, I commit to
> thy will. I am Yours, and I will do my part, as
> You present it to me. You have shown me but
> a taste of Your Glory. I thank Thee, Holy
> One, and I thank Thee, Blessed Mother.

When I finished praying, my daughter and I sat down side-by-side on the grass. The sun shone brightly between the dispersing clouds and the soft, warm wind gently stroked our faces. Everything seemed completely ordinary and mundane. After a few moments of silent contemplation, I put my arm around my daughter's shoulders and hugged her to me. "Tell me, sweet daughter of mine, what did you see here," I said.

She looked up at me and said, "This place has been made very happy, Mommy."

ANNIE EXPLAINS THE LIVING MIRROR

Annie Speaks

The site known as Monk's Mound has deep historical roots and resonates with energy kindled by centuries of prayer and spiritual thoughts even though no one has lived there for hundreds of years. Prayer and devotion generate real power, especially when they become a part of one's being. We have placed people who understand the power of living as prayer in locations around the world to strengthen and maintain this planet's connection to God. Thoughts and words can be destructive, healing, or nurturing, and, once released, they continue throughout infinity. Prayer is the lens that gives clarity to the desires of the heart and brings them into harmony with the will of God. Just as a mirror can direct the rays of the sun to bring light into the shadows, each individual can reflect the frequencies of God to all corners of creation. It is my hope that humans will one day understand this powerful Truth.

To be a living mirror of God is to use thoughts, words, and actions intentionally to spread goodwill to all others. This has nothing to do with positive affirmations. Instead, it requires one to prepare, or "polish," one's mind, body, and heart so that God's energetic frequencies are welcomed and reflected joyfully by words and deeds to all beings. Another action of a mirror of God is to ask to reflect peace in the presence of anger or other destructive energies.

One need not become a yogi, a master of meditation, or a saint to express their spirit being. Feelings of happiness, suffering, peace, mystery, and sorrow help to understand the human condition, and all experiences lead to greater strength.

It is your responsibility to use the compassion learned from your own experiences to elevate yourself and those around you. I cannot state it more clearly or simply. Whatever you need to do to polish your own perfect mirror, do it before it is too late.

***

Thank you, Annie. You explained that concept very well. It reminds me of some of the things I learned from the Native Americans I met while living in the desert out west. I have to say that if it weren't for my friend Cole Eyraud in Desert Hot Springs, I probably would have missed out on all that.

You have formed some excellent relationships with Native Americans, Father. Some of them have gone beyond mere friendship to become more like family. Your association and experiences with the Oglala Lakota and the Flathead people are not just colorful. They are unusual and provide lessons for humans of all races, religions, and colors. I hope you'll be able to share those lessons with this world at some point.

Those are some of the most cherished moments of my life and could fill a book all by themselves—just not this one. I promise that I will write one soon, my daughter, just to make you happy. There are a few points, though, that are relevant to what we have been discussing.

Okay, I'll just fade back into the background and let you have the floor for a while.

The Good Red Road

Over a hundred years ago, the Lakota holy man, Black Elk, spoke of walking the good Red Road. This ages-old Native American concept teaches that virtuous living, respect for and understanding of nature, and recognition and thanksgiving to the Great Spirit or Mystery God,

Wakan Tanka, lead to spiritual strength and renewal.

Many humans these days are spiritually unsettled, and some are drawn to the Red Road hoping to find some meaning in their lives. This is a good thing. The ancient Native American teachings are closely aligned with the teachings and practices established in the early days of Earth by the Creator. That being said, many Native Americans no longer follow those earlier teachings. Many of their beliefs have been distorted over time, just like those of most other people on Earth. So many people have given up on religion altogether while others follow the teachings of individuals and institutions that have no real connection to God, His Spirit, or His Will. They have chosen to follow what the some call the Black Road and are led by hatred, anger, revenge, self-interest, and lack of forgiveness — human emotions that have been at the root of most of the world's problems since the beginning of time.

Human emotions cause damage to all cultures and races on this world. None are immune to the poison of bitterness and unforgivingness. It is foolish to hate an entire group of one kind of humans for what was done to another group of humans hundreds of years ago. How shallow it is for people of one color to hate those of another. How silly is that? Such hatred gains nothing. Millions of White-colored people are aware of the history of Red-colored people and are sympathetic to their problems and needs. The White-colored beings are generously supportive of countless organizations that aid the Red-colored beings financially and help in many other ways to ease their conditions. The majority of White-colored beings alive today have no connection to the things that were done to the Red-colored beings decades and centuries ago. In fact, they generally hold the Red-colored beings in high esteem and with great respect, not because of any guilt they feel, but out of honest love and concern for a culture they have come to appreciate and respect. What was done to the Red-colored beings years ago was, indeed, a terrible thing. Still, a little historical research will show that beings of *all* colors have had terrible things done to them at one time or another and have themselves done terrible things to others.

The issue is not one of color. It is one of humanity. Humanity *must* change, or this world will never be at peace. Regardless of which color being you are, it is not just unproductive to harbor a two-hundred-year-old hatred in one's heart. It goes against the very teachings of the ancient Native Religion, which was the pure and original form of worship on this world. Today, many beings of all colors, in all countries, are leaving their own religions and seeking that earliest unadulterated form. The problem is that it no longer exists. It has been distorted and tainted by the same things that have led so many down the Black Road—human desire and emotion, driven by selfish ego.

The purity can be restored by returning to the ancient ways. The Lakota people use the phrase, *Mitakuye Oyasin*, in prayer. The words in English mean "All my relations" or "We are all related," but they actually mean so much more. It is a prayer that expresses the Lakota concept of the interconnectedness of all things and invokes togetherness and harmony among all life forms—people, animals, birds, insects, trees, plants, rocks, clouds, even between races and cultures that have been at war with each other for centuries. How foolish is it to perpetuate hatred and anger? What does it accomplish? What has it ever accomplished? Only when the element of human emotion comes into the mix is harmony between the beings destroyed. All human cultures are susceptible to the disease of unforgivingness. The Red-colored beings and the White-colored beings are equally responsible for the continued disunity between them. It is time for that to stop. It is time to stop living in the past. It is time to control the baser emotions and bring unity back to this world. Look to the future.

Mitakuye Oyasin demands that hatred of others be dissolved and cast to the wind. Native Americans should lead the world in the healing process, for they hold the design for what was and what should be today. *Wakan Tanka* wants Native Americans to be a light in this world and an example of what True Peace really looks like. They can shine forth as ambassadors of God, but not if they harbor malice and revenge in their hearts. They must radiate nothing but Love. If they do this, God will bless them a thousand-fold. This world needs spiritual *leaders* now, not warriors. Native Americans are the key to bringing all relations back into one unified state of harmony. This is not a statement from a treaty written on a piece of paper and ignored as soon as the ink is dry. It is a Promise from God.

Healing and a Vision of Heaven on Earth

From Elise's Journal

Do you know what it is like to be healed while you are outside of your body? I wish I could have asked my father that while he still occupied his own physical flesh. Pi, who was a doctor, told me many fascinating things when I was a child.

His specialty was psychiatry, but in his practice of helping people work through their mental issues, he led them to explore their spiritual understanding as a means of resolving their internal strife.

Shortly after his retirement in 1992, just seven years before he died, he told me, "You cannot fully understand healing until you get out of the body, Elise. We live in a world where it appears that the body is all there is. As a physician, I know the chemistry and anatomy of the flesh, but I have nothing to do with the source of healing, nor does any other person on this planet. My job has been to speak of what I have learned, and I have used the knowledge where appropriate. I learned that if I were to help the people who came to me with their problems, I must empty myself as much as possible. That is the only way anyone can truly be of assistance to anyone else."

Pi, known as Pacelli here on Earth, was well and widely read. He was also an avid journal keeper. Not long after his passing, I found the several hundred spiral-bound notebooks filled with his thoughts in some dusty old boxes in the basement of one of the houses where I grew up.

Opening one at random, I read one sentence that seemed to sum up the motivation behind his voracious reading and his purpose on Earth. He wrote that he wanted to "… see as much of life as I can so that I may be a good vessel for the healing of all."

What do you do when you see someone you love suffering from a disease that won't go away? That question plagued my mind when I finally learned that the real reason for Pacelli's sudden retirement was because he had suffered a mini-stroke and had been diagnosed with congestive heart failure.

Pacelli was the head of a solid and proud Filipino family. He kept the knowledge of his failing health from most of his family because he did not want to be seen as weak in any way. He also likely believed that he would soon be entirely healed. Unfortunately, he suffered more heart trauma and another stroke that left him unable to speak just a few years after his diagnosis.

He was unable to play his beloved piano and sing his countless songs. He had been an accomplished self-taught pianist and composer and a prolific writer. Almost overnight, these strokes and attacks robbed him of his ability to express himself in these ways. I helped him practice writing preschool words like "cat," "mat," and "sat."

He was at first determined to achieve complete healing, but we all watched as the reality of his failing flesh stole his happiness and drive from him.

✷✷✷

Elise, listen to me now. I tried to tell you so many things back then, but my body would not allow me to speak. But this is not the time to dwell on the past. You need to talk about sound vibrations and healing and the Creation Frequency. Focus now on the vision of healing for all.

You are right, Pi. I will not allow myself to get caught up in the things of the past. Healing can only occur when the noise of the world and the noise of the mind are both silenced.

The only way for humanity to be whole and complete is to connect with God.

Healing energy comes exclusively from God, the only source of true healing on Earth. There may come a time in the future when God's healing power will reach a level and intensity not yet experienced by humanity, but that will depend on humans as a collective. In the meantime, what steps can an individual take to open one's life to The Creation Frequency, and have the healing it brings reflected into the lives of one's family and friends?

First, there must be a conscientious effort to clear one's personal life of noisy clutter so that The Creation Frequency can enter into it with strength and efficacy.

One can begin to heal disconnection from God by first determining if the noise they produce or radiate is helping or harming the perfection of The Creation Frequency. Certain types of music, a TV left on whether or not anyone is watching, and speaking unnecessarily even in conversation all generate potentially harmful noise. The best and easiest way to protect yourself and the Creation Frequency is to limit your noise-generating activities, and the time you spend immersed in the "tech world" of today. People can engage in social media exploration and interaction on their computer or smart device for hours each day without making any audible noise even though these activities generate considerable mental noise. Much of what is encountered in social media, news outlets, and various entertainment venues is overtly negative and obviously harmful. Of equal or greater concern are things that appear to be energetically neutral or even beneficial. It is easy to engage in conversations, play games, listen to the news, or take part in any number of entertainments and pastimes, thinking that they are fun or enriching activities. The danger is that participation in these harmless pursuits can generate a wide range of emotional conflict in a being. One must be on guard so that one's best intentions are not hijacked by ego and become destructive. By controlling external noises, the internal mental noise is made apparent. When the noise of one's personal life is stilled, a reunion with God becomes possible, The Creation Frequency can move freely, and healing energy can flow unobstructed.

There is power in silence. When one makes a genuine effort to experience it every day, transformation and healing begin. Silence is the affirmation of one's desire to commune with the sacred teachings that were heard within the womb and linger in the DNA. Remember how peaceful this world was when it was first created. Remember the beautiful summer days without people, buildings, radios, TVs, smartphones, cars, trucks, planes, political debates, angry voices, and all the other things that generate noise and stress. Remember what it was like to sit under a giant Oak tree at the edge of a flower-filled meadow on that warm summer's day with no sounds other than bird song and leaves rustling in the gentle breeze. In those beginning days, there were no diseases, no war, no chaotic emotions, no tech, no stress. There was only the silence of a perfect planet vibrating peace in its purest form as a perpetual rhythm of worship for a single, omnipotent God Who desired nothing more from His Creation except recognition and love.

The possible consequences of a willful decision to reconnect with God are enormous.

The healing is already here. Ask to know it better in

your life and the lives of all on this planet. Do these things, and heaven on Earth will become a reality.

Touching the Future

When I was a teenager, my mind held a rather romantic image of the future of this world. I spent a lot of time as a boy sitting in my tree house up in a big Pepper tree, a habit I continued through my high school years. Some of that time was spent talking to the "Tree People," as I mentioned in *Volume One*. That wasn't all I did, though. I also did what a lot of kids did back when we had much more of what is called unstructured time on our hands—I daydreamed. That's where many of my romantic images found their genesis.

I have since learned that much of what I dreamed back in those days was more visionary than imaginative. Mary and Annie have both informed me that they were pretty busy "playing with my head" from the moment I exited the womb until some years into adulthood when Mary finally made me aware of her presence. It seems I needed to be given a great deal of information to prepare me to receive the images and instructions that would come later in my life.

One vision I was given while sitting up in my tree house remains particularly vivid. It was a bright and sunny summer afternoon in mid-July. The fern-like foliage of the old Pepper tree that prevented me from seeing much of the sky allowed bright bits of sunlight to come through. The light westerly breeze prompted just enough move- ment among the leaves to create a kaleidoscopic effect of sparkling Blue, Green, and Gold light. It was a beautiful, brilliant, and wonderful sight to behold.

An opening between the branches on the south side

of the tree served as my own personal skylight. I liked to imagine that I was sitting in a planetarium and that the "skylight" was the portal for my daily mental excursions into the Cosmos. I spent uncountable hours, day and night, staring up through that natural opening, watching everything that appeared in the small section of the sky that I called my "uncharted territory." Those were some of the most enjoyable moments of my youth, and the memories linger to this day.

One of those moments expanded into the vision I mentioned earlier. After sitting in the tree house for about half an hour, staring up through my leaf-bordered window, something large and shiny sped across my field of view from right to left. I knew it wasn't a plane because no sound came from it. There was a large regional airport not far from where we lived, so I was accustomed to hearing the rumble of engines when the DC 10s and the little commuter jets took off for parts unknown. I knew it wasn't one of the international jets flying at thirty or forty thousand feet. They look like tiny specks in the sky, and this object had appeared as much larger. It certainly couldn't have been a bird either, unless the bird was wearing a Silver colored coat that reflected the sun.

So, what was it? A UFO? That was my first thought, but my mind didn't hang on to it for some reason. My attention didn't linger too long on the possibility of having seen a spaceship from another world. Maybe *Star Trek* had stretch my imagination so much so that a mere UFO sighting meant very little.

The sighting did trigger a series of daydreams, though. They all had to do with the future and my idea of technology in the twenty-first century.

My daydreams showed me scenes of a spectacular city with giant skyscrapers made out of glass and that had no visible inner support structure such as steel beams or wood. These buildings hovered several hundred feet above the ground where there were lush park lands with grass, trees, running streams, and children playing — a futuristic Shangri-La. There were no cars on the streets, but there were no streets, either, just pathways that crisscrossed through and connected all the parks and gave access to a large, centrally-located lake. Hundreds of people swam in the water or lay or played on the shore in the sun, laughing and behaving like one big happy family.

Colorful flying machines, each one painted with a different design, zipped around the skyscrapers. The people over by the lake looked up at the aircraft, pointing and chatting excitedly as they flew over. Perhaps they were picking out the craft they liked the best. Like the UFO I had seen earlier, the flying machines slipped silently through the air. The only thing these vehicles had in common with the airplanes we know is that they flew through the air, and they were shiny. They were actually what we would call a flying saucer — round, flat with a little bubble or igloo planted in the top center of each one.

The houses of this daydream city were completely underground except for a glass pyramid-shaped structure rising out of the grass over each of them. From my perspective, these pyramids appeared to serve as combination greenhouse-aviaries as well as skylights. I actually saw brightly-colored little birds flitting among the greenery in several of them.

Hundreds of the uniformly-sized glass pyramids scattered about the perfectly manicured Green of the common park made a pretty sight as they sparkled in the sunlight. There were broad stretches of lawn between the dwellings where children played. I watched a group play catch. One of the kids missed a throw. The ball whizzed past him and slammed hard into one of the glass pyramids. I expected the roof to shatter, but the ball just bounced off and rolled into one of the beautiful flower beds surrounding many of the homes.

One of the most notable things about this vision was the total lack of noise. I could hear the children's laughter and regular conversation, so I knew that this daydream came complete with sound. Still, none of it came from booming radios, lawnmowers, or mechanical devices of any kind. I clearly heard the chirping of birds and the rustling of leaves in the gentle breeze — all of the sounds of nature. It was delightful.

I imagined that the year the futuristic city of my daydream might become a reality would be 2000. It just seemed logical to me to believe that all of those changes would be available by then. 2000 was such a portentous number in the calendar of years. It was not just the turn of the century. Nearly every science fiction movie or book I'd seen or read at that time pointed to the year 2000 as marking the boundary between the primitive world and a futuristic world of incredible scientific achievement and modernization. It was the "Magic Sci-Fi Year." Besides, to a kid in the 1960s, the year 2000 was a very long way off.

2001: A Space Odyssey would put the final stamp on the year 2000 as being the year everyone was waiting for. It would be the year when every city in the world would look like something out of an episode of *The Jetsons*. Everyone would be dressed in shiny metallic jumpsuits and eating meals from food replicators. Everyone would have their very own flying air machine, pretty much like the ones I described in my daydream. There would be peace on Earth. No poverty. Dogs wouldn't bite. Disease would be a thing of the past. We would be living in Utopia.

Then something happened that changed my dreams

forever. The year 2000 came, and went. And when it did, I—and a whole lot of other people—were terribly disappointed.

The world really did not look much different in 2000 than it had in 1968.

The cars were a little different, but they were still gas-guzzling, noisy metal boxes. The buildings in my hometown still looked exactly the same, except they were a little bit worse for wear. There weren't any buildings floating hundreds of feet above the ground. Quite honestly, architects hadn't really produced anything all that inventive over the past forty or fifty years. In fact, much of the new stuff was uglier than most of what had been built before 1950. There were even billboards still standing along the highways that had been put up in 1968.

Oh, we did get computers and smartphones, but are they really all that big a deal? They still depend on primitive energy sources and technologies that have been around for many years without much advancement. Every time a lightning storm hits anywhere near where I live, my computer goes off.

I also noticed that people were still pretty much the same in 2001 as they always had been. My friends from 1968 and were now grown-ups. They may have gained some weight and lost some hair, but most still wore Levi's and blue work shirts just like we did when we all bummed around Southern California together. In 2001 we all lived in regular old houses made of wood and cement, and not one of us could buy an aluminum jumpsuit—or wanted to. Most of us lived in cities that really hadn't changed in fifty years or more—except to become noisier, dirtier, more congested, and less safe.

People's attitudes, opinions, and habits, were also pretty much the same or even slightly worse. Tastes and hobbies hadn't changed much, either. Discussion of politics and religion still popped up and sounded just as primitive as when I was twenty years old. Now, though, people seemed to be angrier and quicker to find offense and react with hatred. All the moral anchors like faith, ethics, respect, and common courtesy seemed to be disappearing as well. People seemed to be getting less trusting of each other and nastier about it. Church attendance everywhere and in all denominations, which had been dropping for several decades, took a nosedive after the year 2000.

While some diseases had been controlled or even eradicated by then, many are still out there undefeated. Cancer, diabetes, and heart disease, for instance, continue to afflict more people every year. Don't even get me started on the common cold.

The year 2000 is a couple of decades in the past, and there still are no honest and positive developments on what I call the 2000 Frontier. In fact, it looks like all the hopes and dreams we ever had for a futuristic world of space travel and the incredible technology that comes with a Jetsons kind of world are pretty much kaput. The Space Program has been picked apart and parceled out. The government still runs NASA—sort of. Space X, a privately-owned company, has sent manned flights up to the International Space Station and made some advances in space technology. So far, though, the only activity seems to be sending up rockets and bringing them back down again for reuse. Yes, the good old USA put robots on Mars, but all we have to show for it is photos and the possibility of bacterial life on that planet. NASA is planning to send humans to Mars, as is Space X, but that will still be years in the future. The International Space Station orbiting just outside of Earth's atmosphere has had its ups and downs. Still, they have managed to conduct some simple experiments and send back some pretty cool photos of Earth and of humans floating around inside or working outside in space. I think its highest value is that it is a rare point of cooperation for the increasingly divided and contentious nations of Earth. It is certainly nowhere near becoming the staging platform for interplanetary and interstellar exploration we had all imagined way back in the last century. Oh well, it is a small reality that lends hope to our dreams, so I guess that's something.

Many daydreams linger in people's minds, but the realities are discouraged, underfunded, and stalled at nearly every turn in the road. Most of the tax money humans pay their governments goes to pet projects of dubious value — vaguely-defined social programs, ill-conceived civic improvements, and projects intended to enrich a few well-placed developers, contractors, and government officials. Politicians just don't get it. Humans will never change if all they do is pump money into projects. The only way they will change is if everyone on the planet wakes up one day and says, "Here we are in the twenty-first century, and we're ALL still thinking and acting like a bunch of morons. Why don't we REALLY do something? Let's shake it up a bit. How about we get back to God, quit manufacturing wars, and quit being so ego-driven. Let's dump all the shallow cultural nonsense, get rid of sports, music, and everything else that causes brain freeze in humans. Instead, let's spend our tax money on medical research, healing and protection of our planet, and the exploration of the galaxy!" Fat chance.

As Mary said in *Volume One*, "Humanity should have been dancing on the stars by now." The sad fact is, though, that at the rate humanity is wasting time, energy, money, and resources on foolish pursuits, it will be centuries before anyone from Earth ever sets foot on another planet in this star system, let alone in this galaxy. That saddens me. If that is the attitude of the collective species here on Earth, then The Great Plan of God will end in tragedy for all of them. *Volume One* of *Mary's Diary* made it clear that if a sufficient number of humans did not work together to bring about the changes demanded by The Great Plan, then this world will be judged and declared to be "not worth maintaining."

***

Where am I going with all of this? I'm about to take you on a trip into the actual future. I'm going to give you a glimpse of what reality will be if humanity seriously considers God's two foremost directives and acts upon them before it is too late. As mentioned before, those two directives are:

1. Return to being honestly devoted to God.
2. Clean up the decadent culture of this world and redirect the efforts and energies of society toward goals that have *real* value.

If these directives — okay, call them commands — are not obeyed, Earth WILL be destroyed.

What happens if enough people take those directives seriously and begin to follow them en masse all over this globe? What will Earth become? What will life in the near future be like if humanity is allowed to maintain their colony upon this world under those conditions? Let me remind you of what Annie and I said in *Volume One* about the rewards to humanity if the Strong Weet are joined by the designated portion of humans and meet their Creator's requirements for the survival of Earth:

*The Strong Weet will reveal the ancient civ-
ilization of Annica, and you and I will personally direct the excavation of an archaeological
site that will baffle the minds of everyone on
Earth. Discoveries at this site will bring about
a renaissance in all the arts—painting, sculp-
ture, music, poetry, and the like. The United
States will no longer need to be an agent of
correction using threats to maintain peace
but will be a center of cultural awareness. In
fact, it will be given its original name, New
Annica. A great civilization will arise that will
encompass the globe, and all countries will
become one country. There will be no Third
World. Everything will be hunky-dory.* (Annie,
The Strong Weet Society, page 340)

The cures for all diseases known to mankind
will be revealed in due time. An Energy with
a resonance never before known on Earth will
be released, and in that instant, every person
suffering from disease or illness will be cured.
Regardless of the cause, the new frequency
will rearrange the molecules in every person's
physical body so that illness cannot continue.
It's a simple process, really. I'm surprised Earth
doctors haven't come up with it yet. (Din, *The
Strong Weet Society,* page 350)

The result will be thousands or even millions of years
of peaceful life on this planet if we succeed. The United
States of America will become what it was always meant
to become, a center of perfection and prosperity, a new
Atlantis, and even better, a revival of Annica.

Remember, it is not our intention to leave you in a state of despair but to build upon your hope and to strengthen your expectation for a bright new future for everyone. These books are meant to provide the logical means for everyone to do their part in helping to save this world. This *must* be a communal effort and rise above race, gender, culture, religion, and ego. We are determined to do everything within our power to guide you all into making that a reality, but *you* have to do your part as well.

We have only hinted at what is in store for the future of this insignificant Blue dot at the edge of the Milky Way Galaxy. There is more, but much of it is impossible to explain as The Great Plan was not devised on Earth, and the languages of Earth do not contain the words to describe it.

God's will is for every being on Earth to be healthy and happy, conditions easily understood by humans. If the Creation Frequency is restored to its pure state and The Great Plan is brought to its wondrous completion, health and happiness for all of humanity will be among the first rewards realized.

This planet will become what it was initially designed to be by God—the Jewel in the crown of the Milky Way Galaxy. The Utopian world originally gifted to mankind at the Seeding three and one-half million years ago will be reestablished forever, and no power in all the universes will ever again be able to change it. This and more await those who work with the Weet to repair the eons-worth of damage done to Earth.

The next section of this book has been carefully crafted to stimulate the Awakening of the Weet who have not yet come forward and train them and all other humans who are willing to help bring about the world described in the previous paragraphs.

Guidelines for the Support Weet

The Support Weet are human beings who have read these books, been Awakened by them, and now want to do what is necessary to save Earth from destruction. They may also be individuals who have not read the books but realize that this planet is in serious trouble and want to do something about it.

The original Hectaran Beings who were SEEDED on Earth three and one-half million years ago were called Weet. God had endowed them with gifts and abilities far beyond the capabilities and mundane senses humans have become accustomed to over the years.

If you are either a Secondary Weet or a Support Weet, you carry a portion of DNA code from the Hectaran Founders and are indeed different from the rest of humanity. I must emphasize here that this DNA has nothing to do with color or race. This DNA is spiritual in nature and directs the energic frequency of a Being. One's color or race are irrelevant and have no influence on the expression of the Hectaran DNA. Those who carry this code are Weet, but their personal gifts may vary in strength and ability depending on their relationship to the original Founders. The Strong Weet have the strongest gifts because they are descendants of the ten principle Hectaran Founders, whose DNA was "fixed" before coming to this world and is protected from tampering or dilution.

Let me give you a little personal history before delving into lengthy instruction. It will help you understand this vital information if you know a little of how it came about.

***

Back in the 1970s, I entertained the notion that Earth was in some way affected by the thoughts and emotions of the collective humanity living on the planet. I read an article about how scientists could measure the "weight," or force of thought from the human brain. The study impressed me deeply and led me to think about how human thought output might be one of the causes of air pollution. I reasoned that if thoughts exerted force, then they must have mass. If they have mass, then what becomes of them after they leave a human brain? Is it possible that the thoughts simply float around in the atmosphere, similar to dark matter that fills outer space but is undetectable to human technology? If that were the case, why would it not be possible for the particles emitted by cars, buses, and factories—that is, smog—to be attracted to the thought particles and stick to them like magnets? The result over time would be an accumulation of tons of pollutants floating around in the atmosphere.

Thoughts not only have mass, but they also have energy, and energy has a frequency. Since billions of people think trillions of thoughts every day, why would that energy not interact somehow with the natural, rhythmic energy of Earth? Why wouldn't it eventually interfere with radio waves, TV broadcasts, and other human-generated transmissions? What if human thought energy became so strong and so "attracting" that it interfered with Mother Nature and caused problems with things like the weather and the growth cycles of plants and animals?

Other ideas followed. If human thoughts have that kind of influence, then why can't humans learn to control them? Why can't billions of humans come together collectively and think one exact thought at the same time? That thought could generate a specific and robust energy frequency that could initiate changes for the better in whatever it encounters. Instead of adding to the air pollution with our thoughts, why can't we all get together and dissolve the pollution away? Why can't human beings all over the world decide one day to all go outside at the same time and think, "Cancer be cured"? The human collective could even direct their thoughts into outer space and send out the message, "Here we are aliens. Come say hi."

I wondered why scientists didn't come up with these ideas. Why do they have to keep churning over the same things in their heads, becoming so set in their ways that they can't even consider something if it doesn't fit precisely into their little box or if it doesn't act exactly the way they think it should? Who said everything has to behave in a set and certain way? What if atoms don't act like atoms all the time? Or molecules? What if all the building blocks of this universe are in a constant state of transformation? And what if that transformation can be into anything those building blocks *want* to be? Over thirty years later, Mary revealed something to me that brought those thoughts rushing back:

> *"The energy produced in a nuclear bomb*
> *is an energy that has been forced by the*
> *will of man. How much more would be*
> *the energy produced if the atom were not*
> *forced to split but did so of its own choice."*

That statement made by Mary on page eighty-one of *Volume One* is perhaps the most essential idea she can give to the scientists of this world. *It is the secret to nearly everything!* Think about it, and then think about it some more. Play with it in your heads and then in your laboratories. It is the key.

Those ideas seemed pretty far out then, and I laughed

them off almost as soon as they occurred to me. After many conversations with Mary, though, I realized that most of what I theorized then was actually reasonably accurate. It was what Annie called "the kernel of a brilliant idea." I was not far from advancing to the idea that if energy from human brains can affect our lives in negative ways, then the massive energy output of machinery and all other sources of noise could do the same thing. With the number of these noise generators increasing at such a rapid rate each year, how long will it be before the effects of human "sound waste" becomes evident in the very makeup of planet Earth? How long before gravity is affected? What about the fault lines and regions of volcanic activity that riddle the globe? I'm not talking about the annoyance of simple "sound pollution" here. I'm talking about the potential for damage and destruction triggered by the tremendous output of chaotic energy.

How the Weet Guidelines Were First Conceived

In the early 1980s, while teaching a religion class at a small church in California, I coined the term "Earth Guide" to refer to those in the class who professed to be a "witness for Christ." I assumed that the primary goal of a witness for Christ should be to lead those who do not believe in Christ to a life of faith and belief. I presented this concept to my class and told them that since the church teaches that Christians are "saved" and non-Christians are "not saved," then we are the guides, and they are the ones to be guided. As a pastor in the Christian Church, I know all the jargon, and back then, I used it freely without giving it much thought.

As I dished out my lessons on Earth Guides, I realized two things:

1. These guys weren't getting it.
2. I wasn't getting it, either.

What weren't we getting? Simple. First of all, we didn't really understand the language. The worn-out jargon and clichéd phrases have been tossed around in churches for so long that we have lost track of their true meaning. Terms like "saved," "witness," and "born again" are metaphors used in Christian circles for spiritual concepts that Christians have yet to adequately describe, let alone understand.

The second thing we didn't get—or at least I didn't get—was that my new designation, Earth Guide, encompassed far more than what I presented to the class. I was on the right track, but my teaching was incomplete. An Earth Guide has nothing to do with being a Christian, a Jew, a Hindu, or having affiliation with any of the other organized religions on this planet. Not then, not now, not ever. In fact, it has little to do with the physical dimension at all—which is where religions all reside. An Earth Guide is one who, although housed within a physical form, has more concern for the spiritual plane and with the welfare of things that are spiritual rather than for the material.

When Mary started popping into my head a few years ago, I began to learn what I had been missing. The concerns of an Earth Guide are literally "out of this world," as their work deals with not just physical and spiritual matters but affects interstellar events as well. Worrying only about the physical well-being of this planet and creatures that live on it is no longer a viable option. Earth is a part of a far grander scheme that includes millions of already inhabited planets scattered throughout this universe.

Two significant things occurred in my life that helped me gain focus and a fresh perspective. First, I realized that I had learned all I could from the particular Christian denomination to which I belonged. I wanted insight into the mysteries of eternity beyond what the clichés of any specific group could give me, so I left the denomination and began the Bliss-Parsons Institute. I hoped to teach others what years-long study and personal experience with the heavenly realm had taught me.

Second, with the input of my lovely daughter, Annie, I refined and perfected my concept of Earth Guides, their duties, privileges, and responsibilities. I can now present these ideas critical to the survival of this planet in an orderly and complete fashion.

I no longer use the designation "Earth Guide" but

instead call these crucial spiritual associates "Support Weet" or simply "Weet."

THE NATURE OF TRUE ENLIGHTENMENT AND WHAT MAKES A WEET

A Weet is someone who has achieved a state of personal enlightenment and has made a personal commitment to help other people find theirs.

The word "enlightenment" carries a lot of baggage. Most people use it to refer to the *state of perfection* sought by those practicing certain religions such as Hinduism, Buddhism, or other spiritual and philosophical alternatives to traditional religious practice. In the context of current culture, they are not incorrect, but again, we must dig a little to find the true meaning.

The word "enlightenment" describes the state of being one attains when one "gets it." It is the state we find ourselves in after one of those *aha* moments following an epiphany that strikes suddenly and changes a life forever.

To be enlightened simply means that the lights are turned on. The darkness of the conscious mind caused by misinformation, lies, and indoctrination is replaced by the Light of Truth in that brief and glorious *aha* moment when you suddenly "get it."

So, what did you get? Well, you got several things.

- You got the *Truth* that you are not the person you see every morning in the mirror when you brush your teeth. You are the spirit within the body you see.

- You got the *Truth* that there is no such thing as

race, color, religion, or anything else that separates humanity into divisions or classes that war continually with each other.

- You got the *Truth* that every human being on this planet is a spirit being like you. Everyone is an eternal being of light and energy and connected on a higher level.

- You got the *Truth* that you can't believe much of anything you read in the newspapers, see on the news or the internet, or hear from anyone speaking on behalf of any political party. These agencies are stuck in the physical dimension with no desire to be released. They have chosen to stay stuck because they are rewarded in some material fashion that satisfies their greed, ego, or both.

- You got the *Truth* that you can no longer rely on what your church teaches. The various denominations are focused on pushing their own doctrines and biases at the expense of the Real Truth. I include the many so-called New Age/ New Thought churches and centers. They, too, have become mired in their own doctrinal bias and political agendas over the years.

- You Weet got the *Truth* that most of what goes on here is meaningless. Hobbies, philosophies, entertainment, sports, politics, wars, music, petty differences, habits, attitudes, opinions, leisure activities, human relationships, romances, religions, or even physical life itself—none of it means a thing.

The only thing that matters is Truth. And the Truth is that none of those activities and conventions mentioned in the previous paragraph are true. They are all physical things that come and go and mean absolutely nothing. The Truth is that only those things concerning what comes after life or what lies beyond the edge of this planet's atmosphere have any meaning at all.

If you desire to grow in wisdom and knowledge of the deeper meanings of life and the infinite ways of God, then read on.

If you feel there is more to life than what you see on the television or the internet, you are right.

If you have ever been baffled by the wonder-filled revelations displayed before you in this and the thousands of other universes, then keep your eyes on the stars.

If you feel there is more to life than the "same old same old," you are open to genuine knowledge and wisdom.

If you are beginning to see things through the new eyes of Truth, then I would say that you show all the signs of being a Weet. Continue reading this book, not just for entertainment, but to receive instruction that will prepare you to take part in saving Earth from destruction, not at the hands of an angry god, but from the minds of human beings.

Preface to The Responsibilities and Behaviors of Weet

It should come as no surprise that human beings are expected to be more than what they have become. The road of history is littered with hints. God has withheld nothing from humankind. At the time of their Seeding, the first Beings on this beautiful planet were given the secrets of life and the gifts to maintain health and perfection for eternity. The offspring of those original "pioneers" changed and lost their close and direct association with God. Now, eons later, the Truth of Who God Is has been lost. The image of God that many humans hold in their minds is simply that of a collective consciousness driven by the same emotions and subject to the same fallibilities that afflict all humans. The loss of that knowledge sets up a conflict in the subconscious of everyone. It is only resolved by first admitting the truth of its existence and then doing what God asks.

You have learned so far that you are to be what the Bible refers to as "Stewards of the Mysteries of God" (1 Corinthians 4:1). You have also learned that you have a great destiny to fulfill. You are expected to go out into the world to train others to be stewards. This does not involve knocking on doors or accosting people on the street to convert them to your beliefs, as is the practice in many denominations. You are to lead by example, offering guidance and instruction to gently move others away from the superficialities of this world and onto a path that leads them back to the truth of their heritage and the reality of God.

In the original Greek, "apostle" meant "one who is sent" into the world to do all of the above. Since those four words accurately describe a Weet, then the Weet are modern-day apostles who have been sent to reintroduce God's wisdom and knowledge to this world.

To discover if you are indeed a Weet and have a job to do on this planet, you must first achieve your own enlightenment. This is not as complicated or difficult as many would have you believe. We have previously described enlightenment as having the light of Truth turned on in your mind. When that happens, you can guide others to that same Truth. Enlightenment is not something someone does to gratify their ego. When one becomes enlightened, one doesn't just stop there and sit around in a lotus position all day feeling holy.

We are told that "… you will know the Truth and the Truth will make you free." (John 8:32). When that happens, you are enlightened. You get up out of that lotus position and become an active Apostle of Truth within your sphere of existence. Notice that I did not say an apostle of religion. If the Truth of God is to become evident, then religion must fall to the wayside.

So, if the Truth will make us free, then what are we freed from? The short answer is everything. We are freed from the enslavement of cultural brainwashing, religious bias, learned attitudes and opinions, guilt, fear, politics, peer pressure, what you learned at the university, addictions — the list goes on. Whatever it is that enslaves, you must be released and wholly dissolved by Truth before one is truly made free. If you do not let go of these things, then you will never be free.

What exactly is Truth? Again, the short answer is the realization of who you are and who you are not. You are not a clone of culture or society. You are not a Democrat, a Republican, a Libertarian, an Independent, or a Green. You are not a conservative or a liberal or an anarchist. You are not Yellow, White, Brown, Red, or Black. You are not of any race. These labels are simply artificial designations that do nothing but generate and perpetuate strife and division among humans.

Everyone needs to ignore their egos and wake up. That is what it means to Awaken. You are not the labels others have applied to you, nor are you the attitudes and opinions your ego has collected in your lifetime.

Dear Weet, the *real* you is an eternal Spirit Being, linked energetically to the Beings first placed on Earth. You are a temple of God and a steward of the Mysteries of God.

You are here for a reason.

You are here to Awaken to the Truth of God and to lead others into the light of that Truth. You are, indeed, Earth Guides. It is also your responsibility to generate the proper energetic frequency at specific times throughout the foreseeable future to stabilize the Creation Frequency and repair the damage done to it by the activities of human culture.

The expectations that a Weet must fulfill to guide humanity without becoming like the rest of society fall into two categories—Responsibilities and Behaviors. Only by accepting these conditions will a Weet be able to produce the necessary energetic frequency. This energy will grow in strength and influence as the Weet takes on these responsibilities and establishes these behaviors as part of everyday life.

The list of requirements in both categories is short, and there is nothing mystical or occult about them. In fact, most humans are aware of them on some level, but few ever act on them. If they did, the world would be a much better place. These lists are not just suggestions. They outline behaviors inherent within you but are buried deeply by eons of neglect on the part of all the ancestors that preceded you. If you are to be effective as a Weet, you *must* dig them out and make them a part of your life—a part of who you are.

Most of you who are reading this book have at least a passing familiarity with the Bible. Because of that, I will be using it as a basis for much of what follows. This does not mean that Mary, Annie, and I are Christians in the way that designation is commonly understood these days. We can not follow any of the current Christian denominations—or any other religion, for that matter—because none of them *genuinely* follow Jesus. We do, however, believe in and give devotion to God, the Son, and the Spirit in the way God originally intended by simply acknowledging the existence of God and showing Him commitment by respecting God's Creation.

The Apostle Paul warned that Christians would be lured away from the simple teachings of Jesus, to follow cleverly worded and convincingly taught corrupted versions (2 Corinthians 11:3). Even though some of it has slipped away, the way Native Americans practiced their uncomplicated faith many years ago provides an excellent example for the rest of the world to follow. The Native American tradition of acknowledging the Creator by seeing and honoring His Spirit in all of Creation and every aspect of life is much like what Jesus taught His original disciples.

There is a verse in the Bible that is overlooked or ignored by most people, even those who read it diligently. I bring it to your attention here because it contains a warning relevant to the continuing existence of all human souls. This verse is, indeed, **The Lost Revelation**:

> The time has come for judging the dead
> [all human beings] and for rewarding
> your servants and prophets and your
> saints **and those who reverence your
> name**, both small and great — **and
> for destroying those who destroy
> your earth.** (Revelation 11:18)

The Book of Revelation has been read by countless people at least once, yet no one seems to pay much attention to these powerful words. I have never heard a sermon based on this verse. I have not seen any books or commentaries written about it. I have never seen this scripture reference painted on the forehead of even one football fan. That is why the Weet are here.

Revelation 11:18 makes it clear that everyone will be judged, and everyone will either be rewarded or destroyed. The highlighted portions of the verse define who will get which. Those two distinctions also happen to be contained in God's prime directives and we have accepted the commission to make them known to this world.

You are not God. God *Is,* and you are to not only recognize His existence and presence but show Him your devotion as well.

You must cease producing the kind of energies that distort the Creation Frequency and bring harm and destruction to God's creation.

As harsh as some of the words in this book may seem, this is a book of hope. It is the only book that contains the promise of a wonder-filled future for this world and the exact instructions on how to obtain it. There is no fear on the pages of Mary's Diary. There is only Truth.

Four Responsibilities of The Weet On Earth

1. Feed the Church

In Acts 20:28, the leaders of the early church (who were also Weet) were told:

> Take heed therefore unto yourselves,
> and to all the flock, over the which
> the Holy Spirit hath made you over-
> seers, to feed the church ...

The church at that time consisted of those people who sought for more meaning than was offered by the religions, governments, and society of the world. Those humans were drawn to Jesus because His messages made sense and offered hope to a world that otherwise had little.

The Southern Baptist and Christian Churches of my childhood are famous for their potlucks and carry-in suppers, but that's not what this verse refers to. Scriptures from all religions use the word "food" as a metaphor for thought-provoking ideas and instruction that lead to enlightenment. For instance, Jeremiah 3:15 tells us that "I will give you shepherds after My own heart who will feed you with knowledge and understanding."

Knowledge and understanding are the first two steps toward gaining wisdom. Wisdom is, in fact, the product of knowledge and understanding. Wisdom lies in applying the knowledge you have learned and what you have understood that knowledge to mean for your life.

Too many people simply accept information without questioning either the facts or their source. As a society, we no longer question what we hear, read, or see on TV. We simply nod our heads in agreement and go our merry way. We can be convinced of just about anything, to the point of defending even the most absurd things with our very lives. If this attitude does not change soon, it will be one of the principal factors leading to the destruction of Earth.

The nature of the Weet is to take time to understand the heart of any information presented to them, regardless of the source. They feel the weight of their responsibility to reveal and share the Truth of God. There is no place in a Weet's vocabulary for opinion, attitude, compromise, or agenda merely to appease one group of people or another. Only Truth is acceptable, and no Truth can come from skewed sources. It can only be realized with the guidance of the energetic frequency that connects the Weet to God.

2. Teach

All religions have something like what most Christians call the "Great Commission." The Bible issues this assignment in Matthew 28:18-20:

> [18] And Jesus came and spake unto
> them saying, All power is given unto
> me in heaven and in earth.

> [19] Go ye therefore, and teach all nations,
> baptizing them in the name of the Father,
> and of the Son, and of the Holy Spirit:

> [20] Teaching them to observe all things
> whatsoever I have commanded you:
> and lo, I am with you always, even
> unto the end of the world. Amen

I'm sure some people who read this shy away from terms such as baptism and commandment, but these words have meanings that go beyond what you may have been taught. The Bible becomes an incredible source of power and enlightenment when it is read not from the perspective of any particular faith but rather as a source of Truth understood when contemplated and with an open mind.

There is no confusion as to what "teach" means. Once again, the Bible informs us that followers of Jesus are "… stewards [caretakers, overseers] of the mysteries of God." (1 Corinthians 4:1) The implication is that once a person has acquired knowledge and understanding of Truth, then that person can be trusted to share these heavenly mysteries with others who will treat them with the respect they deserve. In fact, it becomes our duty to do so, as they are not likely to become known otherwise. Regardless of whatever religion you follow or don't follow, the fact remains that there are "mysteries" that need tending, and one should use everything at one's disposal to do that.

A Weet's job is not to teach the same obvious things that pass for spiritual instruction in most churches these days. As these verses imply, a Weet's job is to teach the deeper, more meaningful Truths. We live in a world that desperately needs to hear Truth, but the fact is that most people have no real understanding of what is taught under the auspices of the religion they follow. Many people have been members of a particular denomination since their childhood. They accept at face value the basic tenets of an organized system of belief or, perhaps worse, discard everything they learned in church because of a perceived bad experience. The most profound and life-changing knowledge is never revealed to them because their pastors and teachers do not understand it themselves. These leaders do not lack intelligence. What they lack is the determination to break away from their comfortable belief systems and find real Truth on their own.

I have used selections from the Christian Bible to describe how Weet are to behave and what they are to teach, but that is not the only source of this kind of information. In a previous chapter, I wrote about the old Native American beliefs and practices and how following them can lead to spiritual strength and renewal. There is much to be learned from the words of Hehaka Sapa—better known as Black Elk—and Standing Bear, both of the Oglala Lakota, and Ohiyesa of the Wahpeton Dakota. Their teachings do not contradict those of Christianity but strengthen and reflect them. The words of these Native American Elders shed light on the eternal Truth taught since the beginning of time.

3. Provide Comfort

This is not an admonition to offer people a comfy chair, a warm blanket, and a hot cup of tea. As Weet—modern day-Apostles—it is your duty to provide comfort to all who need it in the most effective and efficient ways available to you. God has given you many gifts to use for this purpose, one of which is knowledge.

Many people need comfort because of the loss of someone close or because of their own impending death. You Weet have the gift of knowing that the essential energy being living inside every human body never really dies but is returned to their celestial home of origin. I briefly mentioned in an earlier chapter the negative influence of the beings from Nibaru and the other dark worlds. One of the saddest lies to poison the human mind, the belief that death is permanent, is the work of these dark beings.

The influence of these dark beings is behind many of the reasons humans seek comfort. It is your duty as Weet to use all the gifts God has given you to comfort those in need. Do not be surprised if you meet with skepticism or even some hostility. The humans of Earth do not understand the true nature of your gifts but do not be discouraged.

4. Take Care of You

You cannot love and care for others if you do not love and care for yourself. You must remember that you are a Weet, a Spirit Being of incredible worth to God whose value cannot be measured.

You cannot be a Weet whose primary purpose is to guide others to Truth if you have omitted or neglected Truth in your own life. And the Truth is that every one of you is precious in the sight of God. Every one of you is here for a reason, and there is no time left to dwell on your faults and failings or to spend hours feeding your ego and molding your image to fit society's standards. God cares little for false, culture-driven self-esteem.

No one is immune to insecurities caused by perceived or imagined personal faults and failings — even the Weet. The answer is to isolate and define the problem, solve it, and quickly move on. Dwelling on these issues over extended periods is counter-productive and leads to ill health. If you have a problem, solve it. If you have a question, answer it. If you have a situation, deal with it. Apply your unique gifts and knowledge to heal yourself, then get back to being Weet. Train others to deal with their issues so that the more significant problems — the lack of belief in God and the distortion of the Creation Frequency caused by this chaotic and misdirected culture — can be solved.

To be effective in this world, a Weet must take care of two things every day. First, establish a healthy diet and lifestyle to keep your physical body strong. The Creation Frequency may be corrected before the end of the time allotted by The Great Plan. However, it may take longer, and in that case, the Weet must remain in their physical forms for the entire span of years and keep their bodies healthy to carry out their duties effectively.

Second, and most importantly, the Weet must maintain constant communication with God and speak to Him daily. The resonance produced when Weet speak is different from that produced by non-Weet. The resonance produced by Weet speech is tuned to the Creation Frequency and merges with it. The co-mingling has the effect of strengthening and correcting the Creation Frequency.

It is not essential, but it is beneficial to set up an altar honoring God somewhere in your home to serve as a constant reminder of who you are. Still, be careful that it does not contain items of a worldly nature. Appropriate items for an altar would be rocks, flowers, shells, a picture of the sun, and other astronomical scenes—perhaps a photo of the Pleiadean system where your home is located. Do not place images of human beings or anything associated with the religions and mythologies of Earth on your altar. God does not recognize any religions or mythologies on this world. He only recognizes devotion to God, the Creator. Yes, Christianity does come close, but Christianity has picked up a lot of baggage since its early days in the way of rituals, catechisms, music, entertainments, costumes, and worldly teachings. Those additions are the constructs of humans, not of God. If you currently attend a Christian Church, that is fine. Church congregations can be like family, and that is a good thing. Just be careful that you don't get caught up in all the worldly extras. Who knows? Your presence and influence might just help guide the congregation back to the "simplicity that is Christ."

If you cannot, or will not, accept these four responsibilities into your life, it will be difficult or even impossible for you to function as Weet. You will not be able to carry out your tasks and fulfill the purpose of your Awakening. No one knows how many ordinary humans and Support Weet must come together out of respect for God to save Earth. If the required portion of the Earth's population does not come forth, then the problems facing the world today—unrest, war, politics, disease, spiritual ignorance, natural disasters—will increase in number and severity. Each of you must accept your responsibilities, acknowledge your gifts, thank God for them, and step up to the challenge.

Make everything you do count for your Creator God, the Great Mystery. Dedicate every thought you think to God. Follow the kind and good leadings of your heart and your conscience, for those come directly from the Holy Spirit. Don't be seduced by whatever is current, fashionable, or popular in society today. Make love and comfort for others the motive behind your every deed. Remember always that the two primary forces in this universe are Truth and Unconditional Love, both of which are lacking on planet Earth. It is up to you to set the stage for their return.

Hello, Father.

Annie! Good to see you. Are you here to write about the Weet behaviors? Did I do okay with the Weet responsibilities? Is there anything you want to add?

No, Father, you did fine. I can take over now if you like.

Please do. I think our readers might like the change.

ANNIE EXPLAINS THE SEVEN PRINCIPLE BEHAVIORS OF THE WEET

Some of you have already Awakened and are aware of your true identity within the scope of eternity. Others are nearly there, and by the time the volumes of this work are complete, the Strong Weet and Secondary Weet will be totally Awake, and hundreds of Support Weet will also be ready to do their parts. Every part is essential. If the Creation Frequency is to be repaired and if humans are to convince God that they want this planet to be rescued, we will need every available Weet. Those of you reading this book who have determined that you are not Weet, please, do not set it aside. We welcome all humans concerned about the fate of this world to join us in our efforts. While you do not have the power of a Weet, you can still contribute a great deal by accepting some of the Weet's responsibilities and emulating their behavior.

We welcome your efforts and accept you as our allies. You will not regret the final outcome.

But hear me now, Weet. The critical job that requires your unique gifts is nothing short of the spiritual revitalization of Earth's civilizations. Literally, *everything* depends on your success. The seven behaviors I will describe have been ignored or misunderstood for a very long time among Earth's various cultures and societies. That ignorance is at the root of every problem facing mankind today.

Things will be different for you from here on out. Situations arise daily that, until now, you have not known how to handle. The knowledge I am about to impart will guide you through them. Pay attention, and you will be prepared to deal with any set of circumstances. That is your job and responsibility as Weet.

You cannot count on receiving any aid or support from anyone on this planet. Other Weet and Support Weet will be glad to assist if they can, but they number very few among Earth's population. That being said, our allies among the non-Weet, are strong individuals indeed and worthy of your love and respect.

First Behavior: Live the Truth

Ask any modern human for the definition of Truth, and you will most likely get some variation of, "Well, that all depends ..." Truth is not an abstract concept to be defined within the context of a situation or circumstance. Truth exists as the absolute and unalterable energetic frequencies that created and sustain the universe.

It is simply a matter of physics that everything in this universe operates according to the Laws of God, Who established those Laws to give you life and wellbeing. Your life begins to suffer when you stray from those Laws. Some of the Laws were discussed in *Volume One* in the sections on the Universal Laws, or Hermetic Principles. Still, there are many other Laws that generate frequencies of great power when used correctly.

You must understand that mere recitation of the words of the Laws is not the same thing as the application of the principles of the Laws to generate the desired energetic frequencies. Words can be manipulated to suit the one who is using them. Specific energetic frequencies cannot be modified in any way without completely destroying the frequency and turning it into something it is not. A word that is a Law of God cannot be changed. It is permanently set for all eternity. Attempts to alter it will not affect the Law, but the one striving to make the change can be harmed in the effort. Fire is always fire. When you were a child, your mother told you not to stick your hand in the fireplace for a good reason. Fire always burns. Humans seem to have difficulty understanding that rule when it comes to the Laws of God.

Four words represent the concepts inherent in Truth:

Faith. There are many things that Faith is *not*. It is not just a word or an emotion. Nor is it the duty of a religious person or simply another word for wishful thinking. Faith is a power source — a tangible substance created from a specific energy frequency that permeates all of creation. The Apostle Paul revealed his understanding of this fact when he wrote:

> Now Faith is the substance of things hoped
> for, the evidence of things not seen …
> through faith we understand that the worlds
> were framed by the Word of God, so that
> things which are seen were not made of
> things which do appear. (Hebrews 11:1-3)

Paul used the term "substance" because he understood a form of physics that had not yet been discovered on Earth during his time. He knew that Faith was more than a word.

Knowledge. The Bible informs us that God created everything by simply conceiving it in His Mind and speaking it aloud. From the mind comes knowledge, and words spoken with that knowledge have power.

Many people alive today have had what is called a near-death experience. These people died, left their bodies for a short time, then returned to life and consciousness in this world. The stories these people tell share many similarities, one of which is having received a command from a higher Being on the other side to be carried out upon return to life. The directive includes the admonition to grow in both Love and Knowledge. Why? Because Love and Knowledge are powerful energetic frequencies given to humanity to use for specific purposes.

Creator. Make no mistake — there is indeed an afterlife. More importantly, there is a Creator, God of the Trinity, The All, God of All Mysteries, Wakan Tanka, Dweller in the Beyond, Who is far more wonderful, powerful, and perfect than you can imagine.

Love. Love, like Faith, is a force. It is an energetic frequency that is beamed onto this planet as a part of the Creation Frequency. It, too, is suffering from distortions caused by the chaotic energies generated by humanity. Real Love — True Love — no longer exists on this planet. It can only be restored if the Weet succeed in healing the Creation Frequency. Every act of kindness and self-sacrifice and every profession of Love to others, whether by Weet or non-Weet, will promote that healing.

The four words — Faith, Knowledge, Creator, and Love — are intrinsically linked to the Creation Frequency and must be regarded seriously if God is to consider a positive conclusion to The Great Plan. Each word contains an element of Truth necessary to the health and well-being of Planet Earth. If the Creation Force that sustains Earth's life is not repaired, God will not renew it. As Weet, you must learn the true meaning of these words and add their power to your own. Learn to display their qualities in your own lives so that others who are not Weet will want to copy them on their own and promote the healing of the Creation Frequency.

Second Behavior: Look for The Good in All Others.

This is something that everyone, not just Weet, should be doing. The effect will be to raise the Love frequency in the people around you, especially those you see often, like close friends, family, and coworkers. Recall the Butterfly Effect—a small action can elicit great response. You may be only one person, but if you alter the behavior of even two or three people and they, in turn, each affect the lives of just a few more, the impact of your action expands exponentially. Now, multiply this by every Weet that has Awakened and you can see how the influence of the behavior is quickly felt around the world. Remember, God does not require *all* humans on Earth to change their behavior, only a certain proportion. If the portion necessary is small, then this could bring us closer to saving the Earth.

Third Behavior: Remind Others of Who They Really Are

This is the behavior of communication. Many of you may not consider yourselves effective communicators, and many of you are shy or uncomfortable talking to others. Weet must be prepared to do things they may not like to do but be assured, you will rise to the occasion. Your knowledge and abilities as Weet will carry you through when the situation calls for it.

In a way, this behavior is an extension of the previous one. Once the good in someone has been found, no matter how small, it needs to be acknowledged and encouraged. Weet need to remind other humans that they are made of spirit energy and are not merely physical bodies with brains. Most people do not realize this and require some convincing. Very few understand that their physical bodies contain enormous energy that gives them the power to create good in their own lives. As people are convinced that their true identity is a spirit residing within a temple made by God, they will be added to the number who are willing and able to assist the Weet in the most critical task ever attempted on this planet.

Fourth Behavior: Practice Healing

A healer is a being who can heal all who come to them, all of the time. That is because God is the only True Healer. A being only has the power to heal if that being truly represents God. They walk among us anonymously and never accept payment for healing those whom God instructs them to heal. Those being are rare.

One effective healing technique that everyone on this planet can use on every person they come in contact with is a simple, short prayer called the "Blessing of the Mind." It should be administered freely to everyone you meet. Don't worry. It does not need to be spoken aloud—unless the situation warrants it. Just repeat these words in your mind:

> Spirit of God, please bless this
> one's conscious mind with love,
> knowledge, and wisdom.

If everyone would do this for every person they meet, it would completely change this world. And, of course, smile. The smile is also a symbol of blessing and has great power when you use it.

Fifth Behavior: Energize the Earth with Prayer

Blanket the entire planet with the same blessing you use to bless other people. Every morning, noon, and night, pray:

> Spirit of God, please bless Earth with the
> energies of love, knowledge, and wisdom.

Never forget that every thought you think and every blessing you bestow brings forth something. Words and thoughts carry energetic frequencies with varying effects on the physical and spiritual worlds, depending on the context and intent. Just as negative thoughts and words generate chaos and damage the Creation Frequency, the words of prayers and blessings bring peace, healing, and reinforcement. They are inspired by devotion to God. Remember that everything is connected to God, and those things that are pure, and give honor to God, will be the most powerful.

Sixth Behavior: Be Devoted to Personal Spiritual Growth

It may be helpful to find a group of like-minded individuals to associate with to discuss your feelings and experiences as your Awakening progresses. You might even schedule a weekly or monthly meeting when you can meet in someone's home to socialize. Be aware, though, that you will meet many who are more concerned with pushing their own agendas than desirous of resonating with a group of Weet. You must not allow them into your circle. Your circle should remain unblemished with the purity of the message of the Diary and The Great Plan, or it will be rejected by God.

Another way to grow is to read books in line with what you have learned since your Awakening. Reread the *Diary*—all of it—and listen to your heart as you consider the words in the context of your own being. Use what you discover to seek out other appropriate books. It would not hurt to read the Bible with an open mind.

Even if you are not a Christian, or if past experience has left you with a distaste for Christians, you will find that the Bible contains wisdom relevant to everyone.

By the way, how do you know if a person is a Weet or not? Just ask them if they've read Mary's Diary. If they have and they love it, they are at least a Support Weet. If they have not read it, you should get them a copy and invite them to talk about it. Anyone who does not like or disagrees with the Diary is not a Weet.

There are undoubtedly other books of a spiritual nature available, but they are few and far between. Be careful how you choose them. Remember that every book written about such things as religion and spirituality is laced with the author's or an organization's agenda, including the book you are reading now. Consider carefully which authors you choose to trust.

Seventh Behavior: Recruit Other Weet

While the number of Strong Weet and Secondary Weet are finite and few, the number of Support Weet is undetermined. There could be hundreds of thousands among the living population of the world today. They only need to be made aware of the need for their help and the urgency of the situation. Again, most of the Strong and many of the Secondary Weet have been identified and begun their Awakening. Still, the Support Weet could be anyone—your neighbor, your favorite waitress, a coworker, maybe even your best friend. Remember that God has determined the minimum number of people necessary to bring about the fulfillment of The Great Plan that includes the continuation of Earth. These are the people who will make up that number.

***

I want to emphasize that while I hope these books have been engaging and fun to read, their intent is *not* to entertain. Each entry in this Diary is not only true but has been carefully crafted to present an essential and powerful lesson. Many of them relate the real-life experiences of Weet as they Awakened and discovered their true identities. As you learn from these lessons and examples, the triggers embedded in each one will prompt your own Awakening, making it easier and faster. This book is a living organism whose frequency will resonate with your own, and the revelation found within these pages will become a part of you and make you think seriously about where you came from, who you are, and where you are going. Who knows—*you* might be one of the Weet still left to be Awakened, and your Awakening might be nearer than you think. It might even have been triggered by this book.

The Final Visitation

The Strong Weet and I are gathered here in the Annica Gardens to give thanks to God for creating us to be exactly who we are. I have known now for quite some time who I am and where I am from, but the other Strong Weet are just now becoming aware of their own incredible reality. They are just beginning to accept their role as Earth Guides and understand what they must do to help save this world from imminent destruction. It was disconcerting for them at first, but they are becoming more comfortable in this new role as the Truth sinks in.

I'm standing at the head of the altar in the center of the garden. I can see the Strong Weet standing with me, one on each side of the altar. Their faces are softly illuminated by the full moon above and a dozen or so solar lights on the ground revealing their expressions and demeanor set with determination to fulfill the expectations and responsibilities placed on them as Strong Weet. The magnificence of their GLOWS radiating for hundreds of feet from each of them is evidence of the immense power of the resources of the Home World they have access to. I have not seen anything so beautiful since the incredible vision described in *Volume One* when Mary turned the backyard into a psychedelic wonderland.

Elise is standing on the north side of the Altar, Her arms straight down at her sides with the palms of her hands turned outward. Her eyes are closed so she can focus her attention on her Hum. It emanates from her just loud enough to create a slight tremor of the Earth beneath our feet sufficient to release the resonance of the thousands of prayers offered at the Altar of Annica over three million years ago. Those prayers were recorded in the rock hundreds of feet below us like music captured in the grooves of an old-fashioned vinyl record. Finally, the record is playing, and the message is broadcast around the world for all to hear:

> *We are here. We are among you. You*
> *are no longer alone. We will call on*
> *you when the time is right!*

Sit stands like a little warrior on the west side of the Altar, her feet apart and her arms folded across her chest. She is gazing up at the moon and reciting an ancient devotional she herself wrote on Hectarus many eons ago. Her mouth moves silently as the words form in her mind.

On the south side of the Altar, Merta stands holding her rosary at her waist. She smiles broadly and each tear rolling down her cheeks falls to the ground by the Altar and bursts into a tiny white flower where it lands.

Each of the three Strong Weet silently employs her own unique gift while I stand in my place on the east side, the head of the Altar. The Hectaran Rock of the Eye is in my right hand, and my left arm extends upward, my palm reaching toward the Pleiades Star System and Hectarus, the giant planet located behind the sun humans call Alcyone.

There had been no hint of a storm, not even a cloud in the night sky, when Elise, Sit, and Merta first arrived at my house. Now, an hour later, the rumble begins. Mother is making an entrance to deliver an announcement. I stand relaxed, open, and ready to embrace the Mystery of what emerges through the sleeping skies of the August night.

The thunder is not typical of an approaching storm.

It is a rippling, rolling current moving through the sky. There is no precipitation, no wind, and no clouds. There are no sounds from crickets, frogs, or other denizens of the summer night. Except for the thunder, the night is silent.

The four of us, alerted by the thunder, stand firm and erect. In the silence between the thunder, Elise murmurs softly, "We are ready, Mother, to receive what You have to tell us."

Then more waves of thunder rolled over us—three in a row, each one more powerful than the one before it. A brilliant ball of White light accompanies the sound. I am reminded of the ball lightning that started my Awakening over a year ago. This time I know what it is and am ready for it. The White light flashes around the Altar in concert with the thunder, growing in size and brilliance as the thunder increases in volume. It encompasses the entire garden as it circles the Altar and fills us with the energy of countless electrons. We feel the flow, but it's not the electric shock from a bolt of lightning. It is the feeling of Mother electrifying and animating a gentle summer night in ways beyond understanding by any human. The three Strong Weet have joined hands and now stand enthralled by the display. Their expressions tell me that they, too, know Who is orchestrating this vision.

We remain standing still and expectant, somehow knowing that the display is not over. Sure enough, one final, booming crack of thunder rattles the windows and foundations of every building and shakes the ground for miles around. For the long minute of the thunder roll, our bodies tingle with the sacred communion She shares with us. We look in unison to the sky above the Altar, and there, just for a moment, we see the face of Mother smiling back at us. We know in that moment that we are not alone and that we have the power of the heavens at our disposal for the completion of His Great Plan.

Now it is over. The GLOWING face of Mother fades away, and the last rumble of thunder is replaced by the ordinary sounds of an August night.

"Now we are six," I say quietly.

"Four more are out there somewhere," Sit adds.

"Some will Awaken as they read this volume of the *Diary*," says Elise.

Then another voice speaks from out of the clear night sky. It is Mary. The fourteen words she utters send chills of excitement and anticipation down our spines:

The revelation is no longer lost.
Prepare now for what is soon to come.

About the Authors

DH Parsons

DH Parsons—educator, inspirational speaker, and spiritual counselor—holds several university and institute degrees and awards, including a master's degree in education and doctoral degrees in comparative religions and transcendental theory. He has taught art, journalism, English, and history in both private and public schools, held positions as both dean of students and administrator in public middle and high schools.

Dr. Parsons currently divides his time between his writing, spiritual counseling, and engagements as an inspirational speaker throughout the mid-western United States.

Elise R. Brion

While Elise R. Brion has earned several university and institute awards and degrees, including a doctorate in religion, she has found her true vocation as a singer-songwriter and inspirational speaker.

Elise is no stranger to miracles of healing, both physical and spiritual and in her own life as well as the lives of others. She shares her gift through recordings of her original songs, and in healing seminars presented throughout the state where she lives.